CANNON'S REVE

Azul brought the blad [illegible] It slid over the soft flesh [illegible] ker's throat. Cut down and through. The pink flesh parted: twin lips of bright red pouted. Blood flowed, spoiling Holly's shirt. Fouling his necktie. The gristle of the windpipe gleamed briefly grey, then was lost beneath the crimson. Azul cut again and the windpipe severed . . .

Also in the BREED series by James A. Muir in Sphere Books:

THE LONELY HUNT
THE SILENT KILL
CRY FOR VENGEANCE
DEATH STAGE
THE GALLOWS TREE
THE JUDAS GOAT
TIME OF THE WOLF
BLOOD DEBT
BLOOD-STOCK!
OUTLAW ROAD
THE DYING AND THE DAMNED
KILLER'S MOON
BOUNTY HUNTER!
SPANISH GOLD
SLAUGHTER TIME
BAD HABITS

BREED: *Day of the Gun*

JAMES A. MUIR

SPHERE BOOKS LIMITED
30–32 Gray's Inn Road, London WC1X 8JL

First published in Great Britain by
Sphere Books Ltd 1982

TRADE
MARK

Set in Intertype Baskerville

Printed and bound in Great Britain by
Cox & Wyman Ltd, Reading

For Gabrielle. Aren't they all?

CHAPTER ONE

The barkeep watched the three men from behind the flimsy shelter of his counter. When he turned away, to stack bottles or rearrange glasses, he watched them in the fly-speckled surface of the yellowing mirror that occupied a five feet by ten feet rectangle of wall. When it happened he hoped the mirror would remain unbroken : it had cost him a lot of money, shipped all the way from St Louis, and it would be near-impossible to replace. That it would happen he didn't doubt. You could smell it in the warm air, an almost palpable feeling of tension, a kind of thickening of the atmosphere, a stretching of time towards the single point, the moment when the fine, tense thread would break.

He wiped sweat from his forehead with the cloth he was using on the glasses. Settled a clean glass beneath the bar. Close to the reassuring bulk of the cutdown scattergun. He paused a moment, letting his fingers run over the smooth, oiled metal, seeking comfort in the weapon. Soon, he thought, it had to come soon. The thread was stretched close to the limit now : soon it would snap. He picked up a fresh glass and began to polish, letting his gaze wander down the dusty room.

One man was seated at the far end, up in the angle of the adobe walls where his back and sides were protected and anyone coming at him had to do it from out front. He had been the first to arrive, climbing down off a big bay gelding that looked to have covered a lot of miles. Maybe as many as the man had years. It was difficult to calculate his exact age, though the barkeep put him somewhere between the late forties and sixty. His hair was grey under a coating of trail dust, and the moustache decorating his upper lip was a pepper-and-salt mixture of brown and silver. There was a stiffness to his movements imparted by saddle-weariness rather than age, and he had paused outside on the boardwalk to stretch his shoulders and back. The barkeep had noticed that he also swung his holster round to the right hip and checked the slide of his pistol against the leather before entering the saloon. His eyes had scanned the room with automatic caution as he stepped through the batwings; clear blue eyes set in a tracery of deeply-ingrained lines that matched the etching of his tanned face. His gunbelt was a plain rig of smooth black leather, the holster a scabbard type with the stuff around the trigger of the .45 Colt's Peacemaker cut away. It looked older than his clothes, but better cared for, as though his priorities set that above personal vanity. In terms of dress the man was neither shabby nor well-dressed. His black pants belonged with the coat lashed behind his saddle, matching the vest he wore buttoned over a plain grey shirt with a black neckerchief knotted loose under the collar. The pants were snug, no loose material interfering with the hang of his gun, and tucked inside black boots. He wore no spurs.

He had ordered whiskey in a deep, quiet voice that carried overtones of authority, and carried the bottle away to the end of the room. The barkeep had noticed that his hands were relatively smooth. Not working hands. The right thumb and the inside of the forefinger calloused.

The barkeep had recognised him as a gunfighter. A pistoleer. And figured him to be passing through: there wasn't anything in Valverde to attract a shootist. Unless he was looking for someplace quiet to hang up his guns. And this one didn't look ready for that yet.

The next man to enter was vastly different, but curiously similar. He was around twenty years younger, with a shoulder-length mane of sun-bleached blond hair falling from beneath a flat-crowned Sonoran stetson that shaded enough of his face to make it difficult at first to recognise him as a halfbreed. He wore a soiled shirt of linen that had once been white, but was now rendered down by washing and the sun to a kind of non-colour. It clung snug across the shoulders and chest, where powerful muscles pressed against the material. It was tucked inside a pair of close-fitting buckskin pants that in turn were worn inside knee-high Chiricahua-type moccasins. From the right moccasin there protruded the leather-bound hilt of a slender-bladed throwing knife. A second knife – a big Bowie – was sheathed on the left side of the man's gunbelt. A Colt's Frontier model revolver hung in a Mexican-loop holster on the right.

This man came in with the same economy of cautious movement as the older pistoleer, checking the room before choosing a table close to the door. When he came up to the counter to get his bottle the barkeep could see clearly the Indian bloodlines in his face; could hear them in his voice. The man's features were of a type a woman might find exciting: good looks combining with a hint of underlying ruthlessness, even cruelty. A man might have seen that face and stepped aside. The eyes were blue, the skin deep-tanned, stretched over wide cheekbones, a strong jaw. His mouth was broad, the lips full and straight; the nose was wide about the nostrils, almost – but not quite – flattened. His voice carried a hint of the guttural tones of the Apache, mixed with the softer strains of a Scottish accent.

The barkeep noted all this and dismissed it: this close to the Mexican border no-one bothered about a man's parentage. Only about the money he had to spend. And the halfbreed had paid in good American coin.

What did strike the barkeep as odd was that two obvious gunhands should happen into the sleepy town at the same time.

And then Jody Garrett came in and the barkeep knew there was going to be trouble.

Jody had been around Valverde getting on three years now. He had come down from Colorado, he said, where he had been a horse-breaker. Certainly, he knew horses:

the outlying ranches sent for Jody when they needed mustangs broken for saddlework. Trouble was, he treated animals a whole lot better than he did people. He had a hairtrigger temper and a big yen to be recognised as a shootist. That temper had gotten him fired from a string of jobs. Once from working as a Wells Fargo guard after he had shot a Mexican he said he thought was reaching for a gun. Other people said the Mexican had been reaching for the money he wanted to deposit. Once from being deputy to Tom Canby when a prisoner had got shot trying to escape. Nothing could be proven, but Canby had said he didn't want a deputy who let prisoners get out of locked cells and pick up a gun. More times from other jobs that had ended in violence. Now Jody hung around breaking mustangs and disappearing every so often into Mexico, or so he said. All that was known for sure was he came back with money.

Jody was not much over twenty, and claimed to have accounted for five men in stand-up fights, not including Mexicans, Indians or blacks. He wore twin Colt's Peacemakers tied down low on both hips, the butts carefully notched with his tally of kills. He hadn't gone so far as to adopt the dime novel idea of a gunfighter's outfit, but he favoured black leather gloves and a dark blue shirt with his denim workpants, and his heels were noisy with the big Mexican spurs he wore.

He favoured both men with a glare as he stamped up to the bar and called for whiskey. He had been out of town the last week or so, and his pockets bulged with money. He threw two drinks down fast, then propped his elbows on the bar and stared morosely at the two men. The barkeep guessed he was deciding which one to pick a fight with.

Some gleam of recognition seemed to show in his yellow-flecked brown eyes, and he tipped his hat back, smoothing his carrotty hair. His attention seemed caught by the older man, for he kept glancing down the saloon as though making up his mind about something.

Every so often he looked towards the door. Like he was waiting.

The barkeep figured he was waiting for Johnny Leroy. The two mostly ran together with Johnny following Jody's lead like a wolf tailing the leader of the pack. The barkeep figured Jody was waiting for Johnny to cover his back. Or maybe just waiting to make sure his friend saw his play.

Either way, it was coming soon.

Johnny came in with a big smile splitting his freckled face and his right hand stretched out ready to grab a glass. He was about the same age as Jody and dressed exactly the same way, except he wore only a single Peacemaker tied down on his hip. His dissatisfaction with the world wasn't anything like his sidekick's, but he went along with Jody anyway. The smile faded fast off his ugly features when he saw Jody's expression, replaced instantly by a look of aggression. He took a drink and followed Jody's gaze.

The barkeep was close enough to hear their muttered conversation.

'You see who that is?' Jody slid his eyes sideways, towards the grey-haired man. 'You see him?'

Johnny shrugged. 'Never seen him before. Who is he?'

'Abe Cannon,' said Jody as though that explained something. 'That's who.'

'The gunfighter?' Johnny swallowed whiskey fast enough he began to splutter.

'Yeah,' grunted Jody. 'They say he's shot upwards o' nineteen men.'

'Christ.' Johnny's face resumed its normal colour as he got the drink down. 'He must be good.'

'I wonder.' There was an edge to Jody's voice. 'I wonder if he's as good as they say.'

'Nineteen men sounds good,' murmured Johnny. 'Nineteen men sounds fast.'

'I'm fast,' Jody snapped.

'Ain't sayin' you're not,' Johnny placated. 'Just sayin' he must be fast, too.'

'Maybe.' Jody poured more liquor. 'He's old, though.'

'Yeah.' Johnny nodded, picking up his sidekick's lead. 'Over the hill.'

'Maybe someone should put him under the hill,' grinned Jody. 'Boot Hill.'

'You?' asked Johnny. 'You gonna call him out?'

Jody shrugged. 'Ain't made up my mind yet. Maybe. Maybe not.'

It took most of the bottle before his mind was made up. He wasn't drunk, but the alcohol had sharpened the edge of his natural temper and there was an ugly glint in his eyes. He called for a fresh bottle and glanced at Johnny.

'Watch my back.'

Johnny nodded and eased into position against the bar so that he could watch both ends of the saloon. The half-breed looked at him. Then at Jody. Then at the grey-haired man. Then he went on drinking, not taking any part.

Jody pushed upright and lifted the bottle. He sauntered down to the end of the room and stood spraddle-legged by the old man's table. The barkeep licked his lips and decided discretion was the better part of valour : the shot-gun could stay where it was. Unless his precious mirror got threatened. The air in the saloon seemed suddenly warmer. Suddenly more still.

'You're Abe Cannon, ain't you?' The bottle dangled from Jody's left hand.

The grey-haired man nodded, not taking his eyes off the redhead's face.

'They say you killed nineteen men,' said Jody. 'That right?'

'What they say? Or what I done?' In the stillness Cannon's voice carried the length of the room. 'There's a difference.'

'Shit!' snarled Jody. 'How many you killed?'

'I never counted,' said Cannon. 'Never seemed worth-while.'

'I shot five men.' Jody sounded proud. 'Face to face. Five men.'

Cannon looked at him for what seemed like a long time. Long enough to make Jody nervous.

Then, 'I ain't gonna be the sixth, kid.'

Jody chuckled. A short, sharp sound. He tilted the bottle to his mouth, then thrust it in Cannon's direction.

'Take a drink with me.'

The grey-haired man shook his head slightly, not moving it enough that he would lose sight of either youngster.

'No thanks. I got a bottle of my own.'

Jody set the whiskey down on the table. Hard enough to slop liquor over the rim of Cannon's glass. He took a step backwards, his knees bending slightly. His hands hung close to his guns.

'You figger you're too good to drink with me?'

'No,' said Cannon softly, 'not too good. Just particular.'

'I could make you.' Jody's voice was harsh now, his intention showing clear in his eyes, in his tone.

'I doubt it,' said Cannon in the same soft voice. 'Walk away. I got no quarrel with you.'

'I'll decide that.' Jody's voice was louder now, pitched to carry so the onlookers could hear. 'I say you'll drink.'

Cannon looked at him. Both his hands were on the table. They rested close to the edge, the fingers spread; loose. He sighed.

'You know something?' he asked. 'I doubt there's a single two-bit town I been in don't have some two-bit kid like you looking to make a reputation. I ain't about to be part of your reputation, kid. And gunning you wouldn't be anything I'd want to boast about.'

Jody's face got darker; redder. His teeth ground together and his mouth thinned out to a taut, ugly line.

'You best back that,' he grated.

'Back what?' Cannon's hands stayed where they were. His eyes stayed on Jody's face. 'You offered me a drink, I refused it. That's all, kid. It ain't the end of the world.'

Jody started to smile again. 'You're scared. Christ Jesus! You don't want to face me. You're scared of me!'

'I watch for snakes, too,' said Cannon. 'I ride round them, too.'

'Some things a man can't ride around,' rasped the carrot-top. 'I'm callin' you out, Cannon.'

The older man went on sitting. Little about him changed, except his back straightened fractionally and a tired kind of hardness came into his eyes.

'I don't want to kill you, kid,' he said. 'I ain't scared of you, but I don't want to kill you. You ain't worth it. Take your bottle and go.'

Now, thought the barkeep, it's going to happen now. He was torn between fear of stray bullets and his desire to watch the outcome.

'Last chance, you goddam coward,' snarled Jody. 'You lift that bottle or you lift yore gun. Whichever way you choose.'

Cannon went on looking at him, not moving.

'I said you're a coward,' snapped Jody.

Cannon still didn't move.

'I say you drink,' Jody baited. 'I say you drink or you crawl outta here.'

When the gunfighter made no reply, made no move, Jody's temper snapped completely. His knees bent and his hands lifted, fisting the matched Colts clear of the holsters. Cannon remained seated. He seemed to shift hardly at all, but suddenly the table was toppling over under the force of his out-thrust left hand and his gun was in his right. Jody's pistols were clear of the holsters, lifting to aim as the hammers came back and his fore-fingers tightened on the triggers. Cannon's gun was already cocked, his thumb dropping clear of the hammer. The Peacemaker bucked in his hand. Once. Jody's guns detonated into the floorboards. His mouth opened in a perfect circle as surprise – disbelief – registered in his eyes. His body jerked back, bending from the waist as Cannon's bullet took him in the gut. It went in just above the belt. Where the skin stretched taut below the ribcage. Where only flesh and muscle protected the belly. It ripped up Jody's intestines and came out of his back in a thick fountain of bright crimson blood. Jody's fancy Mexican spurs jangled as his feet left the floor, then fell silent as the rowels dug into the wood and Jody Garrett pitched full-length into the mess of his own dying.

Up at the bar Johnny Leroy matched his sidekick's gasp and fisted his own gun.

The halfbreed said, 'Don't!'

Johnny part turned, his attention divided for one vital instant. He glanced at Cannon, then at the blond-haired man. And made up his mind.

He spun all the way round, bringing his gun up to angle at the halfbreed.

The man went sideways out of his chair. As he moved, his right hand snatched the Colt's Frontier clear of the holster. His thumb took the hammer back at the same time as his forefinger closed down on the trigger, so that as the pistol levelled on Johnny all that held it from firing was the weight of the thumb. The halfbreed removed the weight before he hit the floor. Johnny's shot splintered panelling on the wall. The halfbreed's bullet splintered a rib and drove through Johnny's heart. It burst the organ into a mess of useless pulp, deflecting off a rear rib to come out just below Johnny's left shoulder-blade. The freckle-faced man crashed against the bar, blood gouting from his mouth and nostrils, splashing over the cleaned glasses. Dripping onto the crouching form of the barkeep. The halfbreed fired again, the second bullet aimed lower. Johnny Leroy grunted and doubled over, not feeling the pain of the lead piercing his belly. He went down on his knees, eyes blanking out as the colour drained from his face. His freckles looked very red and very large. The blood coming from his mouth and chest and belly was brighter. His head lolled forwards until his chin touched his chest, then went on tilting until it touched the floor. He stopped there, his corpse balanced on knees and skull. Wind erupted stinking from between his buttocks.

The halfbreed looked to where the barkeep was standing up. The man had both hands raised, palms out. He was shaking his head and trying to smile reassuringly. The halfbreed nodded and worked the ejector rod to spin the spent shells from the chambers. Dropped in two fresh loads.

'Why two shots?' Cannon came down the saloon. 'He was dead on the first.'

'One's dead, two's sure.' The halfbreed holstered the Colt.

'Yeah.' Cannon nodded. 'I guess. Why butt in?'

'Why not?' countered the blond man. 'He had you cold.'

Cannon nodded thoughtfully. 'I guess he did at that. Time was I coulda taken them both. Now I only get one.'

The halfbreed shrugged without commenting.

'You heard my name,' said the grey-haired man. 'Abe Cannon. Some folks call me Honest Abe.'

'How's that?' asked the halfbreed.

Cannon smiled. 'I always tell a man when I'm gonna kill him.'

The halfbreed grinned back. 'Gunn,' he said. 'Matthew Gunn. Some folks call me Breed.'

'Guess I see why,' said Cannon. 'Buy you a drink?'

'I got a bottle of my own,' said the man called Breed. 'Share it?'

Cannon laughed out loud. 'Sure. I'd be honoured.'

Tom Canby came running in then on the tail end of a big Winchester scattergun. He looked at the bodies and at the two killers, then at the barkeep.

'Fair fight, Tom,' said the barkeep. 'Jody was proddin' an' Johnny went to join in. It was two-on-one until the halfbreed pitched in.

The law officer got his breath back and sucked in his spreading gut. He lowered the shotgun, but kept his finger on the trigger.

'All right,' he said; loud enough for the crowd outside to hear. 'If Mitch says it was fair, then it was fair. They been askin' for it long enough. Trouble is, we ain't accustomed to shootists in Valverde, so I'm askin' you gents to move on. I'd appreciate it if you was outta town come mornin'.'

Cannon shrugged and said, 'I was just passin' through. Didn't aim to stay no longer.'

'The same,' said Breed.

Canby nodded and began to shout for people to get the bodies out. The two men watched them go. The barkeep came out with a bucket and a cloth and began to wipe the blood away.

'Funny, ain't it?' murmured Cannon. 'The other feller picks the fight, but it's us gets told to pass through.'

'Better'n them.' Breed gestured at the bloodstains. 'They just passed on.'

Cannon laughed again. 'Feller,' he said, 'I think I'm gonna like you.'

CHAPTER TWO

Valverde was a small town that looked to have grown piecemeal from the arid flatlands of southern New Mexico. Positioned more or less mid-way between El Paso in Texas and Tombstone in Arizona, its only reason for existence was the spring that fed a constant supply of fresh water to the Wells Fargo depot. The place had begun as a waystation for the stage line, just a low, adobe building that served as a rest stop for horses and passengers alike. There had been a corral and a smithy, and much later – when passengers became more frequent – a genuine two-hole latrine with seats and doors that latched shut when the wind wasn't blowing. By and by, the way station grew. After the War Between the States cattlemen came into the territory, eager to reap the profits promised from the meat-hungry North. The smithy got enough business that it became an independent operation, and then there was a general store. The saloon got built and before long there was sufficient movement through the place to justify a real hotel with an eating house attached. There were enough kids that the townsfolk felt justified in building a school and hiring a guaranteed St Louis schoolmarm to educate them. And Valverde became a real town.

No one knew why it was called Valverde. It wasn't in a valley and it wasn't green, but no one ever got around to changing the name. That stayed the same; like the waystation, which never got any larger, nor any smaller. It just got surrounded by other buildings as the population climbed towards the two hundred mark and people began talking about 'the town', rather than 'the stage shop'. It got itself a peace officer – Tom Canby – who didn't have a lot to do except maybe round up the few Saturday night drunks and ride herd on the cowboys who came in come payday.

The shooting of Jody Garrett and Johnny Leroy was the biggest thing to happen in months. That was obvious from the pointing fingers and whispered conversations of the people who watched the halfbreed and Abe Cannon walk down the single street to the eating house. There was a curious mixture of emotions in their comments, a mingling of approval and fear and hurt pride. No one had ever had much time for either of the dead men, and more than one voice muttered about good riddance. But there remained a feeling that two strangers had ridden in and shot two Valverde boys, which somehow wasn't quite right. No one was prepared to do anything about it, but everyone hoped they would heed Tom Canby's warning and quit town come morning. That way no one would need do anything, except enlarge the story of the shooting until it attained the proportions of a full-scale bloodbath.

'Funny, ain't it?' said Cannon through a mouthful of steak. 'I been hired to clear towns of gun-happy kids like that. An' every time I done what they was payin' me for, they couldn't wait for me to ride on.'

The halfbreed shrugged, accepting the idea with philosophic indifference: he was used to it. Had to be, with the blood of two races coursing in his veins.

'How come you got called Matthew Gunn?' asked the grey-haired man. 'That's kinda unusual for a . . .'

'Halfbreed,' his companion finished. 'Say it. It's not anything I'm ashamed of.'

He began to explain.

His father had been a Santa Fe trader, a Scotsman called Kieron Gunn. He had come to love a woman of the Chiricahua he traded with, a descendant of Mangas Colorado named Rainbow Hair. From his father he had learnt the language and the ways of the *pinda-lick-oyi* – the whites – while from his mother's people he had learnt the skills and harsh disciplines of the Apache. He had been christened Matthew Gunn in the great cathedral at

Santa Fe, but the fierce warriors of Apacheria knew him as Azul, a name given for his clear blue eyes. Breed was a nickname he had picked up along the border country after his parents, his whole *rancheria,* had been wiped out by scalphunters looking for the hundred American dollar reward Mexico offered on male Apache hair. The scalphunters were dead now, all save one: Nolan, the leader. And Nolan was alive only because he was hideously crippled, each moment a torment of suffering far worse than any death. Breed was a name spoken with awe around the Border: some said it spelled death.

'That's some story,' murmured Cannon. 'Which name do I call you by?'

'My friends call me mostly Azul,' said the halfbreed.

'Fine,' said Cannon. 'Azul.'

'You?' queried Azul. 'How'd you get here?'

'Mostly drifting,' answered Cannon. 'I was always good with guns, so I kinda drifted into that line of work. Rode guard on some mule trains. Worked a spell as a lawman. Hired on in a couple of range wars. I never wanted to stop too long in any one place. Except . . .'

A faraway look came into his eyes, and for a moment he was gone to some place inside his mind that only he could see.

'I was married once,' he said slowly. 'A Mexican girl. Had the kind of eyes a man can get lost in. Man I was hunting shot her. I killed him, but it was never the same after that. I got drunk for a long time, then I got real mean for a spell. After that there wasn't much else except what I'd been doin' all along. Now I'm getting kinda old for the work. Like I said back in the saloon: there was a time I wouldn't have needed you to side me.'

'It happens,' murmured Azul. 'Unless you die first.'

Cannon chuckled; cynically. 'I always figgered it'd be that way. I never thought over much about the future. Not until the day I saw it starin' at me.'

Azul mopped gravy from his plate with a hunk of dark bread, waiting for the older man to continue.

'It was the damnedest thing,' said Cannon thoughtfully. 'I was one helluva shootist. Folks talked about me the way they do about that evil-tempered bastard Hardin. I was top o' the tree: one real fast gun. Then I saw I was growin' old. Growin' too goddam old. Down to Texas, it was. A place called Three Forks, up along the Brazos. There was a bunch of kids – like them two we shot – roustin' the place. I got hired on to keep the peace. Not official. Not a U.S. marshal, just the town peace officer. There were three o' them. The wild kids, I mean. You know I can't even recall their names now? But I remember that day like it was just this morning.

'They'd come back into town from wherever they was hellin' it up and settled into the saloon. A bottle was goin' round an' they was boasting about how tough they were. How no goddam grey-haired old-timer was gonna run them out. I went into the saloon an' told them to quit town. Gave them until sundown. They laughed at me. They sat there an' laughed at me an' told me if I wanted them out, I'd have to take them at gunpoint.

'I looked at them an' they looked at me. An' I knew I couldn't cut it. Not against three. I never figgered how I knew: it was just there. I wasn't fast enough no more. Shit! I got faced down, an' that hurt. But all I could do was turn around an' walk away. That felt bad.'

'What happened?' asked Azul. 'What'd you do?'

Cannon grinned. 'I went out of that saloon with my tail between my legs. I walked down mainstreet feelin' lower'n a rattlesnake's arsehole. Then I got me a shotgun an' loaded both barrels with ten gauge. Walked on back to the saloon an' shot the little bastards all to pieces. They looked like jam, drippin' off the walls.'

He shook his head at the memory, chuckling. 'The same day I quit the job. I'd got me some money stashed in Mexico, so I went down to get it. There's a place up in the Utah country I saw once. Silver Wreath Canyon it's called. As pretty a piece of land as any you'll see, an' real good mustang country. Banker named Holly took a deposit on it way back. Said it was mine any time I put up the rest. Now I got the rest, so I'm headed up there. Gonna hang up my guns an' raise me some ponies.'

'Sounds good,' smiled Azul.

'It is,' said Cannon. 'It'll be a whole lot better when I get there. How about you? Where you headed?'

'No place,' said the halfbreed. 'Just drifting.'

Cannon toyed with his coffee. The faraway look came into his eyes and he seemed to be wrestling with a problem. Azul waited for the struggle to cease.

After a while Cannon sniffed and then said, 'I guess I really am gettin' old, but ridin' trail on my lonesome ain't somehow the same no more. Why not ride along?'

The suggestion took Azul by surprise. He had backed Cannon without thinking about it, just butting in when it became obvious Johnny Leroy would kill the older man. It had been an instinctive thing: a reflex action little different to pulling his gun on a snake. He had accepted Cannon's offer of a meal for no other reason than that the grey-haired pistoleer seemed a likeable kind of man, and the dubious animosity of the town threw them together. Riding with Cannon was something that had not crossed the halfbreed's mind. He was accustomed to his own company and felt no need of any other. But he had never been to Utah.

He thought about it.

Finally he said, 'Maybe.'

Cannon nodded. Then, 'I gotta level with you, Azul. I got other reasons.'

The halfbreed sipped coffee, watching Cannon's face. Somewhere deep behind the eyes he thought he saw fear.

'Like I said,' murmured the grey-haired man, 'I'm slowing down. I'll be crossing some rough country with a fair packet of money in my saddlebags. I could use a good man to back me. I'd feel kinda safer with you along. An' I'll pay your way.'

'Money's not important,' said Azul. 'But you said reasons.'

He put an emphasis on the plural.

'Hell!' Cannon stared down into his empty mug. 'I'll level with you. Gettin' old an' the horses ain't the only reasons I'm going. I saw a doctor over to San Antonio a while back, an' he told me I need clean mountain air if I'm gonna live much longer. I got me some kind o' disease that's gonna kill me, I go on living the way I been. Funny, ain't it? You work all your life, you got nothin' to show. Me, I want to breed some ponies before I go.'

He looked up, and now the fear was moved out from behind his eyes to show clear on his face.

'You ever been in Texas with your lungs full of holes?'

Azul shook his head. 'That bad?'

'That bad,' said Cannon quietly.

'All right.' Like joining in the gunfight, Azul said it without really thinking about it. 'Why not?'

A tired smile creased the gunfighter's features. He wiped a napkin over his moustache and sighed. Then he straightened up and the weariness got pushed away, the fear hidden again.

'Thanks,' he said. 'I appreciate that.'

They quit Valverde not long after sun-up. The air was already warm, the sun burning clear out of a cloudless blue sky already bright enough to dazzle the eyes. Tom Canby watched them go, grateful they were departing without further incident. It was a Saturday, and it was the end of the month. That meant the hands would be coming in off the ranches to get likkered up, and the townsfolk would be embellishing the story of the double shooting. Jody and Johnny had never been popular, but there were a few cowboys with a grudging admiration of Jody's reputation. And when they heard the story, they might – after they had drunk enough whiskey – decide to have them some fun. Tom Canby didn't like that kind of fun – it could lead too easily to more gunplay, and Canby liked his town just the way it was. Quiet.

So he watched the old man on the big bay gelding and

the halfbreed on the grey stallion ride out and allowed himself a sigh of relief. It wasn't that he had anything against them personally, he just didn't like having them around Valverde.

He waited until the two figures were lost in the heat haze and then turned towards the saloon, where the barkeep was brewing coffee.

'They gone?' asked the barkeep. 'Where they headed?'

Canby shrugged. 'They ain't goin' nowhere. They're just leavin'.'

CHAPTER THREE

They rode northwest, moving on a line that held the Dragoon mountains on their left. Ahead of them lay the Gila river, and then the headwaters of the San Carlos. Lordsburg was over to the east, but the first settlement of any size they would encounter was Fort Thomas, built in a curve of the Gila.

It was familiar country to Azul, the high, wild fastnesses of Apacheria. It was Indian country, the domain of the Apache, and not yet conquered by the steady encroachment of the *pinda-lick-oyi.* That eventually it would be taken from the tribes, he did not doubt. That was the whiteman's way: to take with the strength of their guns, their superior numbers, their organisation, what they had little use for. The old stories of the Chiricahua told of the time of the first people, of the first Apaches who had come down from the north into a land so rugged, so desolate to those who lacked the vision to see its beauty and its bounty, that it was a country no one wanted. The Apache had made it their own, holding it against Navajo and Comanche, against Ute and Mexican. But not against the *pinda-lick-oyi,* who came out of the East like the waters of the ocean Azul had once seen washing remorseless against the shore. There was silver in the hills, some copper; to the southeast the land was good for cattle, so the whiteman claimed it for their own. Men like Kieron Gunn saw the beauty of the terrain and the nobility of the savage warriors who claimed it, and sought only to live in peace with the redmen. But he was an honest man, a straightforward man, simple in his desires. Most, Azul knew, could not accept the presence of Indians, believed with a fervency that approached fanaticism that theirs was the right to take, to drive the Apache out. Already there had been fighting, and there would be more, for the tribes – at first content to live alongside the whites – fought back with the ferocity that had made them legendary.

Azul could understand both sides of the ugly coin. His mixed blood set him that vital bit apart from whites and Indians alike that he could view the running war with a curious objectivity. On the one hand, he could understand, though without accepting it, the desire of the *pinda-lick-oyi* to *possess* the land. To build upon it and fence it in; to divide it with roads and railtracks; to establish forts as protection against the wild raiders who struggled to retain their freedom. And he could see – and understand better – the Apache need to live free. To wander with the seasons, not owning the land, but living in harmony with it. To hunt and fish and fight. It was a glorious freedom that he knew was in irrevocable conflict with the desires of the newcomers. And, equally, he knew that the whitemen must inevitably win. But it was a victory that would be hard and bloodily fought; that, too, he knew.

And now he rode through that harsh, sun-baked land, conscious of the danger. Ahead of their path lay the country of the Be-don-ko-he, to the east the territory of the Chi-hen-ne. Southwest were the Ned-ni, and due west the Chi-e-a-hen. His own people – the Cho-kon-en, or Chiricahua – claimed that area through which they now passed, and even further to the north were the White Mountain Apache. The names were those of the people themselves; a whiteman would have spoken of Mimbreños and Jicarillas and Mescaleros and Warm Springs Apache, but Azul thought of them in the tongue of his mother, the language of his childhood. They were his people, and to ride again through their domain imparted a feeling of coming home; of being again in a place where he belonged.

'I guess having you along is a kind of safe ticket,' said

Cannon. 'You bein' part Apache.'

Azul laughed, shaking his head. 'Maybe not. Maybe they won't like me bringing a whiteman through here. A *bronco* sighting down a rifle won't ask me who my mother was. He'll just see two whites with guns he can use riding good horses. That makes us both fair game.'

'I figgered they'd let you pass,' Cannon frowned. 'I thought the Apache didn't fight their own.'

'Mostly they don't,' grunted the halfbreed. 'But why'd you think Indians would be so different to whites?'

'Hell! I never thought much about it,' shrugged the gunfighter. 'Guess I don't know that much about Indians.'

'Whites fight each other,' said Azul. 'They didn't, you wouldn't be here.'

'That's right,' acknowledged Cannon. 'I never looked at it that way.'

'Whitemen don't,' Azul murmured. 'Not often.'

After that they rode in silence, Cannon suddenly more cautious.

It was strange, Azul thought, that a man so used to violence would have so blind an attitude to the Indians. But then Cannon was not an Indian-fighter. His life had been mostly lived around towns, hiring out his lethal expertise to the highest bidder. It was a savage life, lived never very far from death, but it was a different kind of savagery to that ruling these hills. Like most *pinda-lick-oyi*, Cannon tended to lump Indians together in an amorphous mass, knowing only that there were different Indians in different parts of the country. Assuming that all Apaches, or all the Sioux, were a single people rather than a loosely-allied collection of sub-tribes, each with its own territory and its own customs, each member of the sub-tribe an individual. It was a common mistake, and one that could lead too easily to death.

So Azul rode with his eyes scanning the terrain ahead, wary for signs that might indicate danger.

The country got higher and wilder as they moved northwards. The flatlands gave way to foothills and then to the full grandeur of the mountains. The trail Azul had picked took them up on a winding path into the high reaches of the Black Mountain country. Cactus gave way to timber, the slopes thickly wooded with pine and juniper and cottonwood. Deer watched from the safety of the thickets and high above crows wheeled, stark against the blueness of the sky. The air was warm, filled every so often with a swirling cloud of white as a random breeze shook loose the seeds of the cottonwoods. They crossed lush mountain meadows and deep, shadow-filled arroyos; streams gurgled, foaming white across their path; and all around them there rose cliffs of striated rock, shimmering in rainbow hues under the dry sun. Oak and maple and aspen added colour to the timber, shades of green and gold and silver mingling with the whites of the cottonwoods and the banding of the rock to produce a kaleidoscope effect that was breathtaking in its magnificence.

'You know,' said Cannon as they topped a ridge and paused, staring out over a canyon filled with colour, 'this is one helluva country.'

Azul just nodded, watching a spiral of buzzards descend across the blue to a point hidden by the trees. Whatever pickings the birds had spotted lay directly in their way. And the presence of the scavengers, not yet come down to feast, indicated a recent death.

He drove his heels against the flanks of the big grey stallion and went down the slope, his right hand never moving far from the stock of the Winchester sheathed alongside his saddle. Cannon, too, had seen the birds and recognised their meaning. He began to draw his own rifle.

Azul caught the movement and said, 'Don't. Just ride easy.'

'There's something dead down there.' Cannon sounded confused by the halfbreed's warning. 'I never did take to ridin' into trouble empty handed.'

'It's maybe not trouble,' grunted Azul. 'Whatever did the killing's not around. Else the buzzards wouldn't come down.'

'Might be someone's layin' up there,' argued the gunfighter. 'Ready to pick off anyone comes lookin'.'

'Might be,' allowed Azul. 'That's the case, then we play it as it comes. You go in with your hands full, you could stay bare-headed.'

He grinned as Cannon reached involuntarily to touch his hair. Where a scalping knife would make the first cut.

'Safest thing's to show we're peaceable,' he murmured. 'Peaceable, but ready.'

Cannon shrugged and took his hand away from the rifle. He didn't look like he enjoyed it, but he followed the halfbreed's orders without further argument.

Down at the bottom of the canyon the trees gave way to grass that was dotted with juniper and willows. Bright scarlet flowers grew along the banks of a narrow stream. Azul reined back inside the treeline, hugging the shadows as he checked the ground ahead.

The grass was trampled down in a line that bisected their own trail. The blades were not yet sprung upright again, indicating the recent passage of several ponies. Close to the water there was a larger area flattened, an extension of the trampled line running out into the trees on the far side of the stream. At the centre of the wider trampled area there was a man. He was naked, and his wrists and ankles were lashed to branches driven into the earth. Blood showed, bright as the scarlet flowers, on his chest and thighs. His eyes were closed and from the corners of his mouth there ran lines of drying saliva. He was moaning softly, just loud enough to keep off the buzzards that were now landing around him.

'Jesus!' Cannon kept his voice low. 'What the hell's this?'

'I don't know.' Azul's reply was a low rumble of sound, not loud enough to carry beyond the splashing of the stream. 'Whoever put him there will be watching.'

'What do we do?' Cannon asked. 'Cut him loose?'

'Not if you want to reach Utah,' rumbled the halfbreed. 'There'll be a reason for it.'

'Christ!' Cannon stared at the criss-cross pattern of cuts

decorating the man's chest. Ants were crawling over the lines, and the air around the man's groin was black with flies. 'We can't just leave him.'

'You don't, you join him.' Azul pointed up the canyon. 'We try to ride around, we'll be climbing for maybe three days. You touch him and you'll be either dead, or worse off than him.'

'Worse?' Cannon gasped. 'There ain't no worse'n that.'

'You're fresh,' said Azul; almost casually. 'You'd have longer to think about your mistake.'

'You're a hard bastard.' Cannon's voice held a grudging admiration. 'You don't give a damn.'

'I don't know him,' said Azul. 'Why should I?'

For a moment it looked like Cannon might argue it, but then he shook his head and said, 'All right. We're in Indian country, I guess. An' you're the Indian.'

'That's right.' Azul took off his hat and draped the stetson from his saddlehorn. 'You ride out slow and easy. Stay behind me and don't do anything less'n I move first.'

Cannon nodded, watching as the halfbreed wound a bright red bandanna about his hair. Dressed in the faded linen shirt and Chiricahua moccasins, he looked now more Apache than white. Had the mane of sun-bleached blond been dark, he could easily have passed for a full-blooded Indian. He took the grey horse's reins in his left hand and walked the big stallion out into the sunlight, his right hand open and far away from his weapons. Cannon followed nervously behind.

Azul rode down towards the staked man with the prickling warning of impending danger tingling down his back. The buzzards saw him coming and took fright, lumbering into the air with a heavy beating of wings and a raucous protest at the interruption. The man opened his eyes. They were glazed, red from staring into the sun. His tongue extended from between his lips, stroking dry over the parched surfaces.

'Help me.' His voice was a faint, pain-wracked grumble. 'For God's sake help me.'

Azul ignored him, reining in just clear of the body.

This close up, the wounds looked worse. The work of experts. Knives had been drawn over the man's flesh in a series of carefully-placed cuts, rending the skin so that it bled and stung with the man's own sweat, but not deep enough to bleed him to death. He had been castrated, but the flow of blood from between his legs was stemmed with an application of mud and grass. He was badly sunburned, blisters puckering the pale skin of his chest and belly and legs. The sound of the stream so close must have been a separate agony.

Cannon said, 'Jesus Christ!' very softly. And it was difficult to know whether he was blaspheming or praying.

In the language of the Chiricahua Azul called, 'We come in peace. We ask you to let us pass.'

A voice answered from the trees beyond the stream. 'Who are you?'

'I am called Azul,' he replied. 'I am of the Cho-kon-en.'

'You have white hair,' said the voice. 'The hair of a *pinda-lick-oyi.*'

'My father was a whiteman,' Azul called back. 'My mother was Rainbow Hair. Daughter to Mangas Colorado.'

'I have heard of you, Azul.' The voice remained wary. 'Who is the whiteman with you?'

'He is called Abe Cannon. He is a stranger to our country.' He put a slight emphasis on the *our*. 'I am riding with him to the Utah country. To the mountains beyond the Painted Desert.'

There was a long silence. The buzzing of the flies seemed to get louder. The staked man went on moaning, his words indistinct. Azul waited, feeling the tension ease a little: had the Apaches hidden in the trees decided to kill him, it would have happened by now.

Then a man stepped into view. He was short and heavily-muscled. A black vest decorated with tarnished conchos covered his chest and he wore moccasins that were a match of the halfbreed's. A dirty white loincloth hung down almost to his knees, supported by a belt that held a long-bladed knife and a Cavalry model Colt. His hair was long and black, shiny in the sun, held off his flat-featured face by a leather war band. There was a single-shot Henry carbine in his hands.

'I am called Enjuh,' he said. 'Because I am very bad.'

Azul smiled at the joke : in the language of the Apache, *enjuh* meant *good.*

'I think the one called Cannon is sick,' grinned Enjuh. 'I do not think he likes what we have done.'

'I do not think this one likes it, either.' Azul inclined his head towards the moaning man.

Enjuh laughed : a good sign.

'He came looking for silver,' he said. 'He offered weapons and bullets to the man who would guide him. One agreed, but he was a very foolish Indian : he trusted the *pinda-lick-oyi.* He took his woman with him, a good-looking woman. When he had shown the *pinda-lick-oyi* a place where there was a little silver, the whiteman shot him. Then he took the woman. Like the Indian, he was a foolish whiteman.'

'Yes,' said Azul solemnly. 'A stupid whiteman.'

'He had two friends.' Enjuh sounded almost sad. 'We killed one when they tried to run. I am sorry he died so quickly. The other one is hiding somewhere. We thought he might come to help his friend.'

Azul shrugged, not speaking. Waiting.

'Tell this to the one called Cannon.' The way Enjuh said it, the name came out Kah-non.

Azul turned in the saddle, translating for Cannon.

'Smile and nod your head,' he finished. 'He's testing you.'

'Never did have much time for rapists.' Cannon spoke through a huge smile, nodding vigorously. 'But that's one rotten way to die.'

Azul said nothing, just turned back to face Enjuh.

The Apache stood silent, watching Cannon's face. After what seemed a very long time he said, 'You may pass in peace. I think I will let this one live to tell the other whites what happens to *pinda-lick-oyi* who take our women.'

Azul nodded and urged the grey horse forwards. As he passed, the man on the ground followed him with his eyes. There were tears there.

'Go fast,' warned Enjuh. 'I do not want to scare off the other.'

They rode across the stream and into the trees. The Apache faded back into the shadows and the woods fell silent again.

'My God!' said Cannon. 'I never seen anything like that before. Why didn't you at least shoot the poor bastard? I coulda taken the Indian.'

'There were nine of them,' grunted Azul. 'Anyway, he deserved it.'

'How'd you know?' Cannon demanded.

'I saw them,' answered the blond-haired man. 'And Enjuh wasn't lying.'

Cannon's face was pale. He spat as though trying to clear his mouth of a sour taste. 'Poor bastard,' he repeated. 'What a hole to get himself into.'

'She didn't invite him,' grunted Azul. 'He had it coming.'

Cannon got paler, but he didn't say anything more.

CHAPTER FOUR

That night they made camp in a grassy clearing surrounded by oak trees. A ridge bulked across their way to the north and behind them the ground sloped down to the canyon. The place where they had seen the man staked out was hidden by the timber. They watered the horses and left both animals hobbled, free to crop the luxuriant grass at will. The land was quiet, lit by the pale radiance of a near-full moon. From the ridge ahead a wolf howled, and somewhere lower down the slope a bobcat screamed once. The leaves rustled as a faint, warm breeze blew from the south, drifting the smell of frying pork over the clearing.

Azul and Cannon rested on their saddleblankets, drinking coffee. The natural tranquillity of the place came close to dispelling the tension that had grown back in the canyon.

'Tell me something,' Cannon asked. 'What would you have done if I'd put that poor bastard out of his misery?'

'Tried to stop you,' Azul replied.

'Be difficult.' Cannon chuckled. 'I'm still fast.'

Azul shrugged. 'You'd be dead if you'd tried.'

'You?' asked Cannon. 'Or your friends back there?'

'They'd have killed us both.' Azul reached forwards to lift pork from the pan. 'Way they see it, trying to interfere would be like trying to stop a hanging.'

'That was a damn' long way worse'n any hanging,' grunted Cannon. 'That was torture.'

'He raped an Apache woman.' Azul's voice was flat, hard. 'He shot her man. He did it in Apache country. He suffers the Apache way.'

'When in Rome,' murmured Cannon, 'do like the Romans do.'

'Where's Rome?' asked the halfbreed.

'Someplace called Italy,' said Cannon. 'It's an old town.'

'I never heard of it.' Azul began to chew on the pork.

Guess there's things we both don't know,' said Cannon thoughtfully. 'Things we both hafta learn.'

'If you want to reach Utah alive,' Azul nodded.

Cannon grunted and helped himself to meat. They ate in silence. Azul had already dismissed the subject from his mind with the pragmatism typical of the Apache. The dying man had broken the laws of the Chiricahua. His offence had been against the Indians, therefore it was up to the Indians to punish him. That Apache justice was savagely direct was a thing he should have considered before chancing its wrath. He had opted to take a chance and now he was paying the price. That was all: it was not a thing worth dwelling on.

Cannon, in turn, was wondering what kind of a man he had joined up with. No stranger to death himself, he accepted its possibility; indeed, he had lived long enough under death's shadow that it was an accepted part of his life. To gun a man the way Azul had back in Valverde, that was understandable; that was justified. But to leave a man to die that way, that was something else. It was a facet of the halfbreed's nature Cannon had not seen, had not anticipated. It was the Indian blood: the harsh acceptance of suffering, what appeared to be a careless disregard for life. Or at least for the dignity of a man's dying. That the man had deserved to die Cannon didn't argue with. He would have shot him without a second thought, certainly without feeling any remorse. But he wouldn't have made him suffer that way first. That wasn't Christian. And then he realised that he wasn't thinking about Christian people, and Christian people did some pretty unpleasant things themselves, so maybe it really was a case of accepting the rules of the game and adopting the same attitude as the halfbreed. At least Azul had got them through the canyon alive.

But deep down Cannon knew that he could never think

the same way. Could never fully agree with Azul's attitude to life.

The moon shifted across the sky. The breeze died down and the air got still. They poured the last of the coffee and banked the fire.

'Best we keep a watch.' Azul canted his Winchester across his legs. 'I'll go first.'

'Sure.' Cannon nodded and eased back until his head was resting on his saddle. 'Wake me when it's my turn.'

He closed his eyes, feeling sleep near by. His final thought was that he really was getting old. Time was, he wouldn't have been so ready to give way to weariness.

Azul sat listening to the night. Now that Cannon had stopped talking he could hear the life all around him, the night-time noises indecipherable to ears not trained to hear them. Something old Sees-The-Fox, the Chiricahua hunter who had taught him so much, came back to him.

'Most men see only a little piece of the world,' the old man had said. It had been on a night like this. A warm, clear night, high up in the Mogallons, where the old man waited with the fourteen-year-old boy, teaching him the ways of the Apache. *'It is like looking at a tree. There! That one. What do you see?'*

Azul had followed the old man's pointing hand and stared at a juniper, silvery under the moon. *'I see a juniper,'* he had said. *'I see its trunk and its branches. There are leaves. It is an old tree, and once it was struck by lightning for I can see the scar on the bark and a place where a branch was torn loose.'*

'You see part of it,' old Sees-The-Fox had said. *'As much as I would expect you to see, for you are young and your eyes are good. And you learn well. Now be silent and listen to the tree.'*

Azul had listened, knowing that there was some reason for the lesson. The night had been very quiet, and as he concentrated he found that his ears told him things his eyes could not. He was not sure how long he sat there listening, for his concentration was so total that he forgot time, but after a while Sees-The-Fox had woken him from his listening and asked him what he now knew about the tree.

'There is a bird nesting there,' Azul had said. *'I hear it moving in its nest. Therefore, there must be two birds, and if one is on the nest there must be eggs. There is a bees' nest hidden in the branches, for I can just hear the bees. A snake sleeps by the trunk – I heard it move. It makes a different sound to the leaves.'*

'You see?' Sees-The-Fox had smiled in the moonlight. *'There is so much more than just a tree, but to see all of it you must use all your senses. To know a thing properly, you must use your ears and your nose and your fingers as well as your eyes. And even then you may not know it all. That tree has roots under the ground: a part of it that is always hidden from us. The roots may be healthy or rotten. Perhaps some are broken. Some may burrow through stone while others find an easier way. Even though you watch that tree and listen to it, you cannot know it all. And there are two lessons learnt from that. The first is that even when you cannot see a thing, you can still know what happens about you through the messages of your ears and your nose and your skin. The other is that the tree is like a man: no matter how well you know him, there is always a part you cannot see. A part that is always hidden from you. And that part may be as you expect it to be, or it may be rotten. You may never know, for it is a part that shows only when the tree is torn loose from the ground.'*

Azul remembered those words as he sat in stillness, listening to the night and thinking with part of his mind – the part not tuned to the world about him – of Abe Cannon.

And then a sound that was not part of the natural order intruded. It was a rustling that had nothing to do with the movement of animals. It was too clumsy for that: the kind of sound a man would make if he was trying to hide, but was not accustomed to moving with the silent stealth of an Apache. Azul's thumb tightened on the Winchester's hammer. His forefinger took up the trigger slack. He glanced at Cannon's supine form. Wrapped in his blanket, the grey-haired man was deep in sleep. Azul faked a yawn and climbed to his feet. Like a man bored with the long watch through the quiet hours of the night. He paced leisurely across the clearing to where the horses were standing. Moved around them as though checking them. And faded into the trees.

He moved with the silence of a warrior closing on an enemy sentry, his moccasins noiseless on the soil. His nostrils flared, almost like an animal's, testing the night air for the scent of danger. Whoever was approaching the camp was not, he guessed, an Indian. A cautious man, sure, but not an Apache. There was too much noise for that. And too little for the approach to be friendly. He moved on through the trees, his breath controlled, his passage taking him through those parts of the timber deepest in shadow.

And then he saw the man.

He was tall and thin. Hatless, the moon glistening on a skull partially bald, surrounded by a fringe of hair that descended into a thick beard. The man's shirt was torn and there was blood on his face and hands where twigs had scratched him. The knees of his pants were torn and dirtied, as if he had crawled on hands and knees. There was a gunbelt around his waist and a Smith & Wesson Schofield in his left hand. He was standing inside the tree-line, watching the clearing through wide, frightened eyes.

They got wider still as Azul came up behind him and smashed the barrel of the Winchester down against his wrist. He yelped, dropping the gun, and spun to face the halfbreed.

Abe Cannon came awake at the sound. For an old man he moved fast, rolling clear of his blanket with the Peacemaker coming up in his right hand to point at the source of the disturbance.

'Azul!' he called. And the halfbreed was impressed to

hear him say it quietly, not raising his voice so that it would carry beyond the clearing.

'Visitor,' answered the halfbreed. 'Coming in.'

He prodded the man with the Winchester, driving him out onto the grass. Cannon stood up.

'What the hell is this?'

'Oh Jesus! Thank God you're white.' The man stumbled towards Cannon, clutching his damaged wrist. 'I thought you might be Apaches.'

'Why'd that worry you?' Azul demanded.

The man looked at him like he was staring at a crazy man. He shook his head, turning towards Cannon.

'They jumped us,' he said. 'Me an' my partners. Three of us. We'd heard talk of there bein' silver up in the Black Mountain country, so we figgered to try our hands prospectin'. The injuns was friendly at first. Said they'd give us a guide. His name was Hosco, near as I could tell. Bastard tried to steal our horses, but we caught him at it. I guess we got kinda mad. Leastways, we beat up on him some, then let him go. The goddam injun brought his brothers back, an' when we made a run fer it they come after us. Strother got killed along the way. Then me an' Ike got separated an' I been wanderin' around since. Lost my horse goin' down an arroyo. Damn' animal fell, an' when I got back on my feet it was hightailin' it outta the place.

'Christ! I'm glad I run into you gents.'

Cannon nodded and dropped his Colt back in the holster.

'What's your name?'

'They call me Lefty. Lefty Dwyer.'

'You tell us the whole story?' Azul kept the Winchester pointed on Lefty. 'You left any out?'

Lefty frowned. Then shook his head vigorously.

'Nossir! Happened just like I said. Why?'

'Ike,' asked the halfbreed. 'He was a big feller? Lot of brown hair?'

'Sounds like Ike,' agreed Lefty. 'You run into him?'

'We saw him,' Azul nodded. 'Dying.'

Lefty's face got pale. 'They caught him?'

Azul nodded again, not speaking.

'Poor bastard.' Lefty sighed. 'Leastways I made it out. Real piece o' luck runnin' into you two.'

'Maybe,' said Azul. 'It depends.'

'I don't get it.' Lefty swung his head to stare at Azul, then back at Cannon. 'They ain't on my tail no more, if that's worryin' you.'

'Not that.' Azul shook his head.

'Well, hell.' Lefty started to grin. 'There's three of us, an' we all got guns. You let me fetch that ole pistol an' loan me some shells, we can handle the goddam injuns.'

'You already handled one,' rasped Azul. 'The way I heard it.'

Cannon said, 'You reckon he's the third man?'

'He said it,' grunted Azul. 'He has to be.'

'I don't understand.' Lefty turned from one man to the other. 'What you talkin' about?'

Cannon glanced at Azul, who shrugged and said, 'Tell him.'

'We come across your partner,' said the gunfighter, 'down in the canyon. The Apache got him staked out. They figgered you might come lookin' for him. They want you on account they say you raped the guide's woman an' shot the guide. What you got to say about that?'

Lefty grinned, exposing a row of tobacco-stained teeth. 'Hell!' he said, 'we had us some fun with her, sure. She wasn't nuthin' but a goddam squaw. I seen 'em peddlin' it around the tradin' posts, but she wasn't puttin' out. All we wanted was a bit o' somethin' in the night. Woulda squared it when we hit the silver, but her man got mad. Bastard tried to take us on, all three o' us. We beat him up like I said, but then Ike figgered we'd best shoot him lest he told the others. Damn' woman got away then, an' she musta made it back to her camp because the next thing we knew, there was goddam injuns all over.'

He screamed as the stock of Azul's rifle slammed into his back. The blow pitched him forwards, off balance, so that he stumbled and fell down on his face.

'Christ!' he groaned. 'She wasn't nuthin' but an injun bitch.'

'My mother was a squaw,' said Azul; slow and cold and deadly. 'I'm part Apache.'

All Lefty Dwyer said in reply was, 'Oh my sweet Christ!'

He got up on his knees, his hands stretched out to Cannon. He looked almost as though he was praying. His breath came in short gasps, and there was moisture forming in the corners of his eyes as a thin stream of spittle ran from his parted lips. He shook his head slowly from side to side, as if trying to rid himself of a bad dream.

'What the hell do we do now?' asked the grey-haired man.

'Give him to Enjuh,' grunted Azul. 'It's what he deserves.'

'No!' The tone of command Azul had heard back in Valverde was in the gunfighter's voice again. 'We can't do that.'

'*We*?' said the halfbreed.

'Me,' answered Cannon. 'I can't let you do that.'

Azul stared at him across the fire. Dwyer was between them, still on his knees with his eyes fixed firm on Cannon's face. The gunfighter ignored him, his own gaze locked with Azul's. In the moonlight the lines on his face looked deeper etched, like cuts. His hair shone almost silver. His stance was relaxed, arms hanging by his side. His right hand was close to the butt of his Colt and his mouth was set in a determined line.

'He deserves hanging,' he said, 'not what they'd do to him. No one deserves that.'

Azul saw the determination in his face and knew that this could end suddenly. Bloodily. He had no doubt that he could beat Cannon if it came to a fight: even allowing for the awkwardness of the Winchester in a close-up shoot-out the rifle was out and ready while Cannon still needed to draw. Crazily, Azul wondered how it would be if they were both using handguns. He could understand Cannon's reluctance to hand the man over to Enjuh and his braves. And knew at the same time that by his own code that was all he could do: Dwyer had violated an Apache woman; killed her man. It was for the Apaches to punish him as they saw fit.

'Don't force it,' he said. 'I'll kill you if I must.'

'Yeah,' said Cannon. 'I think you would. Try, at least.'

'Not try,' said Azul. 'Do it.'

'He's not worth it,' said Cannon. 'Let him go. Let him take his chances alone. On foot.'

'No.'

Azul's reply was final.

'I can't let you do it,' said Cannon. 'I have to stop you.'

Azul stood with the Winchester loose in his hands. The muzzle was angled down, pointing at a spot between Dwyer's feet. All that was needed to line it on Cannon was a slight upwards movement. All that was needed to plant a .44-40 calibre slug in the gunfighter's belly was to cock the hammer and squeeze the trigger.

Azul didn't want that. He wasn't sure why. It might have been the sheer bravery the old man was demonstrating in the face of what had to be certain death. Or it might have been that Azul's mixed blood let him see Cannon's side of the argument. He didn't want to kill Cannon, but he knew that he couldn't let Lefty Dwyer go free.

Cannon stood, deceptively casual, his body turned slightly so that his right shoulder was towards the half-breed. That way he presented a slightly narrower target. He looked tired and determined and dangerous. And Azul knew that he was ready to back his words with gun-play, even at the cost of his own life. That alone was a point in his favour. A point Azul could respect.

'All right,' he said.

And lifted the Winchester, squeezing the trigger.

For the instant of the rifle's firing muzzle flash illuminated the clearing. The report echoed off the trees sending birds, roused from sleep, fluttering and squawking through the branches. The slug took Lefty Dwyer in the back. It hit just above his pelvic girdle, breaking his spine and deflecting off to the right so that it tore through his stomach to exit from the front of his body. Sparks gouted from the fire where the bullet landed, sizzling as Dwyer's blood pumped out in a thick stream. The man jerked up and back, his face distorted in agony, his mouth stretching wide over his stained teeth as an awful wracking cry came from deep inside him. He fell down on his side, back arching at an impossible angle as his fingers dug deep into the soil, ploughing furrows that were bloody where his nails tore and broke. The scream died down to a strangled gargling sound and he began to twitch, involuntary muscular action twisting him in a circle that left the grass flattened and bright with the outpourings of his back and belly. His head beat crazily against the ground and his legs drove hard in a curious running action, as if he sought to push himself away from the pain.

Across the fire Cannon had the Colt in his hand. His mouth was open in an expression midway between a snarl and a gasp. His eyes, at first furious, slowly widened in surprise. He stared at Azul, then at the wounded man. He said, 'Christ!'

Azul levered the Winchester, sending the spent shell case arcing bright in the moonlight across the clearing. He kept the muzzle pointed on the gunfighter.

Dwyer performed a full circle. The grass under him was slick now with blood. The gargling was changed to a deep-throated groaning gasp. His lips were stretched far enough back that his gums were showing and his teeth ground together. All the blood seemed to have drained from his face, the paleness emphasising the hollow sockets of his eyes. The front of his shirt was drenched, plastered against his bony ribcage. His bowels opened, urine spreading in a dark stain across his groin and thighs; his pants got dark and stinking. Somehow he got his hands under him and pushed upright from the waist. The motion opened the wound in his belly wider, sending fresh spraying from the exit hole. His legs ceased their movement, hanging limp and useless. He stared into the fire with eyes glazed over, sightless in their agony.

Cannon let the Colt droop in his hand. He squeezed the trigger.

And Lefty Dwyer's skull exploded like a pumpkin hit with buckshot. Pieces of bone and sticky grey brain matter fountained over the grass. Blood pulsed from the hole, running down Lefty's face, into his eyes and his mouth. Where the bald patch had been there was now just an emptiness, in which the moon gleamed briefly on jagged edges of bone, loose nerve endings, the pulpy stuff that had once been his brain. The gasping stopped abruptly, Lefty's jaw falling slack. His body relaxed, flopping onto the grass like a puppet with its strings cut. He seemed smaller in death, deflated. Some black-winged night insect buzzed through the stillness that followed the two shots, landing delicately on the rich pickings of Lefty's opened skull.

Cannon flipped the loading gate of the Colt open. Drove the ejector rod back into the chamber to shove the expanded cartridge case out. Fetched a fresh shell from his belt, and thumbed it into the Peacemaker. He snapped the loading gate shut again and dropped the gun into his holster.

'I guess that settles it,' he said, very softly so that it was hard to know just what he meant. 'It's over.'

'No.' Azul shook his head. 'Not yet.'

'He's dead.' Cannon looked at the corpse with an expression of distaste. 'He got what he deserved.'

'Enjuh might not agree.' Azul let the Winchester's hammer gently down.

'Enjuh ain't around to discuss it,' grunted Cannon. 'Enjuh can go to hell.'

'He'll be here,' said Azul. 'He'll have heard the shots.'

'So we pull out,' said Cannon. 'We got a head start.'

Again Azul shook his head. 'He'll want to know what happened. We go now, he could come after us. You want to run all the way to Utah?'

'How the hell can he find us?' Cannon demanded. 'We can be long gone.'

'Through Apache country,' said Azul. 'He can send word ahead to stop us.'

Cannon frowned, confused. 'How?'

Azul dropped the Winchester on the grass and drew the Bowie knife. He held the big blade in his right hand, turning it so that the fire was reflected from the polished steel. He turned it so that the reflected glow played on Cannon's face, and then he passed his left hand back and forth over the blade.

'Like that. Soon as the sun's up.'

'A heliograph!' Cannon was surprised. 'You mean they send mirror signals? I thought that was just the Army.'

'We've used them a lot longer.' Azul sheathed the knife again. 'Long before the Army.'

'You live an' learn,' murmured Cannon.

'No,' grinned Azul, now the moment of tension was passed. 'You learn first, that way you get to live. Up here, at least.'

'Guess I got me some learnin' to do,' said Cannon.

Azul shrugged. He picked up the rifle and set it on his blanket. Then he went over to the nervous horses, murmuring softly, calming them. Cannon took hold of Lefty's feet and dragged him over to the edge of the clearing. Already the black-winged insect had been joined by others. The first buzzed irritably at the disturbance.

'Now what?' asked the gunfighter. 'Don't reckon we'll be sleepin' much.'

'Not you.' Azul stretched on the blanket. 'You're on guard now.'

Cannon stared at him as he closed his eyes and let his body relax. 'Don't nothing bother you?' he asked.

'Not him,' Azul said, looking to where the corpse lay.

'We did him a favour. You could say we saved him from a fate worse than death.'

'Jesus!' Cannon spat into the fire. 'You really are a hard bastard.'

Azul settled himself more comfortably on the blanket.

'He got into this with a bang,' he murmured. 'He just went out with a bang.'

CHAPTER FIVE

Abe Cannon sat watching the sun rise and boil the mist off the woodland. Over to the east the sky was already bright, the big, pale yellow disc shining out of a silvery blueness that promised another hot, dry day. The brilliance chased night's shadow westwards, transforming the canyons and arroyos and ravines from gloomy, menacing darkness to the rainbow hues of day.

It did nothing to dispel the darkness gnawing around the edges of Cannon's mind.

He looked across the clearing to where Azul was checking over the horses, thinking that the halfbreed showed more concern for the welfare of the animals than he did for human life. The business with Lefty Dwyer had taught Cannon a lot about his companion; had brought home the intrinsic hardness in Azul's character. That Dwyer had deserved killing Cannon didn't argue with. Couldn't after the man's careless confession. But handing him over to Enjuh and his warriors to suffer the same lingering death as Ike was something that went against the grain of the gunfighter's nature. His thinking, his attitudes, were shaped by his experience, and that experience was gained from dealing with whitemen, from messing in whitemen's problems. Two men might face up to one another in a dusty street or a fly-blown saloon and only one would walk away, but that was quick. The quick and the dead. Condemning a man to hours – days – of agonised suffering was alien to Cannon's nature. And a natural part of Azul's.

It was, Cannon realised, the difference between them. Azul's attitudes were those of the Chiricahua who had raised him. At the core of his being there was that innate cruelty: that typically Indian disregard for life as whitemen saw it. And Cannon was, he knew, essentially a product of what he thought of as the civilized world. Azul was not. He was not purely Indian : he was educated in the ways of the whitemen, could move amongst them as one of them, but there remained that part of him that set him forever outside the bounds of so-called civilisation. And that difference was now opened between them like the split of some deep, dark high country ravine.

Abe Cannon had been born in Kansas. His parents had worked a small farm, barely large enough to support themselves, let alone a fast-growing boy with a penchant for wandering. He had quit the farm – with few real regrets – when he was sixteen years old. His father had given him a horse and a Colt's Dragoon, with a sack of powder and two pouches containing percussion caps and lead balls. Abe had headed straight for Ellsworth, where his build and his natural talent with hardware had got him a job as bouncer in a cathouse. He had killed his first man there. A cowboy with sand-coloured hair and a Patterson Colt belted cross-draw style. His name had been Charlie Ivers, Cannon remembered. He couldn't recall many of the men who had followed Charlie Ivers into the endless sleep, but the cowboy's face had always stuck in his mind. Ivers had got mad at one of Madame Fay's girls. No one ever knew what about, if there really had been a reason. There had just been the screaming, and Madame Fay hollering for Cannon to get up the stairs and sort it out. He had burst into a room that stank of sweat and whiskey and sex. And seen the cowboy using one of the big, sharp-rowelled spurs he favoured on the girl's face and breasts. There was a lot of blood on the dirty sheets and the girl's screaming had rung in Cannon's head so damn' loud he could hear it now. He had the Dragoon out ready in his hand. Had laid the barrel hard across Ivers' skull. Hard enough to put the crazy cowboy out. Not soon enough to save the girl from permanent disfigurement.

Ivers' ramrod had settled up with Madame Fay: they agreed that forty dollars would cover the damage. Ivers – when he came to – was told his wages had been docked. That even more than the turkey-egg bump on his skull had made him mad as a bobcat in a cage. He had come looking for Cannon. Had found the youth and called him out, confident that he could beat a kid. He had lost. And Boot Hill had gotten one more cheap marker. The trouble had been that Ivers had friends, and they had come looking for Abe Cannon. He had quit Ellsworth with thirty dollars in his pockets and the knowledge that his conscience wasn't disturbed by killing.

He had drifted over to Abilene and picked up with a muleskinner called Tobe Hooper, a Texan who boasted of a taste for human flesh. Most of Hooper's talk was pure bluff, a load of bravado put up to camouflage his basically decent nature. He had taught Cannon a lot, and paid him enough that the youngster was able to purchase a seven-shot Spencer carbine. They had gone down the Chisholm Trail to San Antonio, where Hooper got drunk one stormy night and fell off his mule hard enough to crack his skull. Cannon had found him and got him to a doctor, who bandaged the fracture but couldn't do much about the pneumonia. Hooper had taken a long time dying, and after Cannon had supervised the burial and sent what was left of Hooper's money – less his own wages – to the man's family in Las Cruces, the youth had got himself work riding shotgun on a stage. That had lasted over a year before he signed on as a deputy in a border town called San Ysabel.

He had been a good peace officer, but his steadily growing reputation had brought too many hardcases into town looking for a fight, so he had drifted northwards. He had worked in the Indian Nations and guarded silver in Colorado; drifted up to Wyoming, then down to Utah. The same problems had pushed him south again, down into Arizona, then into Mexico. He had been a bounty hunter and a marshal, worked as a bodyguard for a

French nobleman visiting his Mexican estates. Along the way the old Colt's Dragoon had gotten traded in for a Navy Model Revolver, and all the time his legend had grown. He had ignored the passing of the Civil War, knowing nothing of the South and totally unaware of the slavery problem, let alone the deeper economic issues. He had killed more men and got himself married. His wife had been shot – as he had told Azul – and he had spent the better part of two years hunting down her killers. The Colt's Navy had been replaced with a Peacemaker and the Spencer with a Winchester. Not much else had changed, except his hair had begun to turn grey and sleeping rough left him a little stiffer.

Then he had noticed that every so often he found himself short of breath, and that sometimes there was a sharp stabbing pain in his chest. He put it down to age and the bullets dug out of his body, and did his best to ignore it. Until one day it had hit him harder than ever and he had found himself on his hands and knees in a Tularosa hotel room with the pain sparking lights over his watering eyes like someone had clubbed him. The nearest thing Tularosa had to a doctor was a barber with a way of tending sick horses. Cannon had gone over to San Antonio feeling more frightened than he could remember. The doctor had diagnosed something with a long and incomprehensible name in a language he had said was Latin. All it meant to Cannon was that he would die choking on his own blood if he didn't quit the saloons and dusty streets that were his habitat and get up to Utah to claim his right to Silver Wreath canyon.

That had always been the vague idea in his mind ever since the death of his wife. It had been a kind of dream, a kind of insurance policy. Mexico had gone sour on him since Maria was killed, and he had paid only one last visit. Spent a morning arranging to take his money out of the bank and the afternoon saying his farewells to the marble headstone that was his wife's last link with life.

And then he had gone back over the border towards Valverde.

And now he was riding with a halfbreed killer as ready to consign a man to torture as a child would slowly pluck the wings from a fly.

He looked at his horse. The bay was in its prime. So far the journey hadn't even come near taxing its strength. It could outrun any goddam Apache pony with wind to spare. But Cannon didn't know this country. He didn't know Indians, and what he had learnt so far warned him that getting out of these hills in one piece wasn't just a question of his horse's speed.

And when it came down to the bare bones he had to admit that Azul had compromised. He had shot Dwyer himself, sooner than fight with Cannon. That had to mean something.

He massaged the ache in his left shoulder, cursing time and what it did to a man, and poured coffee. Azul came over to the fire with an armload of wood.

'We got enough,' said Cannon.

Azul set the branches on the flames. They were green and rapidly sent up a thin streamer of smoke that rose undisturbed in the still air.

'Sign. To guide Enjuh in.'

Cannon shrugged and began to scrape a straight-edge razor over his jaw.

'You take hair?' he asked. 'Apaches?'

'Sometimes.' Azul hunkered down, satisfied with the smoke signal. 'It depends.'

'On what?'

The halfbreed shrugged. 'On if we want it. If we got time.'

'I saw Cheyenne up along the Bozeman.' Cannon felt his fresh-smooth cheeks and wiped the razor dry. 'They carried hair on poles.'

'Coup sticks,' said Azul. 'They'd most likely keep scalps to remember the battle. To show how brave they were.'

'An' Apaches?' Cannon asked. 'You don't?'

'No.' Azul drank coffee like a man with all the time in the world. 'What hair gets lifted is shown off, then burnt.'

'Them.' Cannon pointed to where Lefty Dwyer was starting to smell. 'Will Enjuh take their hair?'

'No.' Azul's face was calm, as indifferent as if they were discussing the merits of a good horse. 'There's no honour in that.'

Honour? Cannon thought. He's talking about honour? After the way Ike was staked out? After they cut him like that?

Azul must have read his expression for he said, 'White-men get medals, don't they? You get hired to keep the peace and when you kill someone doing that you get praised. Some Army officer takes his men in on a village and wipes it out, he gets a medal for it. He's a hero. I've seen soldiers using tobacco pouches they cut off Apache women. I've seen the women's bodies.'

Cannon thought about the girl back in Ellsworth. After she had seen what Charlie Ivers had done to her face she had hung herself.

'That don't make what they done to Ike right,' he said. 'Not killing a man that way.'

Azul shrugged, 'What would happen in a town? To men like that?'

'They'd get hung, I guess. Maybe sent to prison.'

'Some Indians believe hanging traps the soul.' Azul poured more coffee. 'You ever been in prison?'

'No.' Cannon grimaced. 'I couldn't take that. Not bein' locked up.'

'Nor could an Indian.' Azul looked hard at the gun-fighter. 'At least Ike got a chance to show how brave he was. To die with some honour.'

'That's how you figger it?' Cannon asked; genuinely interested now. 'Kinda like a priest askin' if a dying man regrets his sins?'

'Something like that.' Azul emptied his cup and

climbed to his feet. 'It gives a man a chance to show how he's as strong as his killers. How he can ignore pain. That way he dies with some credit in the Spirit World.'

Cannon nodded thoughtfully. There was something in that. Not necessarily anything he could really understand yet, or anything he could agree with, but something. It wasn't, he decided, as black and white as it seemed. Or in this case, as red and white. There was an awful lot he didn't know about Indians. But he had a good teacher. And he was getting his lessons first hand.

The day was still a long way off its full heat when Enjuh appeared.

Cannon guessed he was coming from the way Azul stopped honing the throwing knife he carried in his right moccasin and stared at the trees.

'Leave me to talk,' ordered the halfbreed. 'Just follow my lead.'

'How'd you know?' Cannon asked.

Azul looked vaguely surprised at the question. 'Listen.'

Cannon listened. Then shook his head, 'I don't hear a thing.'

'That's it,' Azul said. 'The birds have stopped singing.'

He hunkered down by the fire, refilling the coffee pot. Cannon went on listening, abruptly conscious of the absence of sound. The woodlands were silent, the background noise stopped. Instinctively his right hand touched the familiar contours of his pistol. He glanced at his rifle, propped against his saddle with a shell ready in the breech. His mouth felt dry, the way it did when he knew he was walking into a fight. He hawked and spat, seeking reassurance in the action. He wasn't afraid – or rather, he had long ago learnt to live with his fear; to control it – but there was something approaching the uncanny in the way Azul seemed to know what was going to happen before the event.

Then he heard the sound of ponies coming through the trees.

'How'd you know it's him?' he asked. 'Not someone else.'

Azul grinned tightly. 'He's not hiding his approach. He's seen the smoke and he's coming to find out what it means.'

Enjuh came out of the timber on the far side of the clearing. He was riding a heavy-chested mustang with a single rawhide rein and a pad saddle. The old Henry was canted over the pony's shoulders. He halted just clear of the trees, waiting until Azul invited him to dismount.

'There is a smell of death.' He spoke again in the language of the Chiricahua. 'I heard shots in the night.'

Azul poured coffee, handing the mug to Enjuh.

'The other *pinda-lick-oyi*,' he said. 'He came into camp last night. He asked us to give him shelter. We killed him.'

Enjuh nodded, swilling coffee around his gums. 'We?'

'We,' Azul confirmed.

'The man called Cannon shot one of his own?' Enjuh sounded doubtful.

'Yes,' said Azul. 'I shot him with the rifle. Cannon shot him with his pistol. He took a long time dying.'

'That is good,' said Enjuh. 'Though it is a pity you did not give him to me.'

'We are going to the country called Utah,' said Azul, 'we could not know you were still waiting.'

'But you put up sign,' said the Apache. 'You waited this long.'

Azul shrugged. 'There was time to wait for a brother. Even though the one called Cannon is in a hurry.'

'Whitemen are always in a hurry,' said Enjuh. 'They scurry about like ants. But it is good that you waited. Good, too, that Cannon joined you in the killing.'

Abruptly he stood up. Cannon watched him go over to the body. He turned it over, ignoring the cloud of flies that erupted from the congealed blood, from the ruin of Dwyer's skull.

'It will be difficult for him to think in the Spirit World,' he said. 'Whose bullet did this?'

'Cannon's,' Azul replied.

Enjuh grunted, drawing the long-bladed knife from his belt. He went down on his knees, grasping the front of Dwyer's pants. He hacked through the belt and ripped the material apart, dragging the trousers down around the corpse's ankles. Cannon stared with a mixture of fascination and horror. The knife's blade glittered briefly in the sunlight as Enjuh took hold of the testicles and penis. Then it became dark as he slashed the edge against the soft flesh. Through the soft flesh. He raised his hand, displaying the ghastly trophy. There was a murmur of approval from the Chiricahua standing round.

Dwyer's mouth was still wide open, fixed by rictus action in that last dying cry. Enjuh thrust the testicles into the hole. The penis, rigid in death, protruded from between the parted lips. Enjuh stood up.

'It is good,' he said solemnly. 'Let him walk through the Spirit World with what he did showing on his face.'

Insects, attracted by the new opening in Dwyer's body, began to gather. Soon the man's thighs were dark with ants and beetles. Flies clustered afresh on his face, concentrating now on the mouth.

'Go in peace,' said the Apache. 'I will send word ahead of you that you are both friends of the Chiricahua.'

Azul nodded, not replying as Enjuh swung astride the mustang. '*Ugashe!*' he called. 'Let's go.'

As swiftly and as silently as they had come the Chiricahua faded back into the trees. The birds began to sing again. Azul doused the fire and began to saddle the big grey stallion. Cannon picked up his own gear and stowed it on the bay.

'That's it?' he asked. 'That's all?'

'That's all,' nodded Azul. 'You did good.'

'Thanks.' Cannon swung into the saddle, glancing down at the obscene disfigurement of Dwyer's corpse. 'Leastways I did better than him.'

'Yeah,' said Azul. 'He really ballsed up.'

CHAPTER SIX

They moved on, riding steadily north and west. The Chiricahua ranges faded behind them, Apache Pass on their left hand, the Gila ahead. Mostly they slept rough, living on the game Azul brought in. Twice they spent nights in Apache *rancherias*, where Cannon drank the fierce home-brew called *tiswin* and tasted for the first time real Apache food. He was surprised it tasted so good.

He could see no difference between the Indians offering them hospitality and those of Enjuh's band, but Azul said these were Be-don-ko-he, friendly only because Enjuh had sent word to let them pass unharmed. In the second *rancheria* they sat long into the night with a squat, cheerful warrior who clearly loved to talk as much as he loved to drink. He boasted in a mixture of Spanish and American of his battles, and gave his name as Goklya. The next day Cannon asked Azul what *Goklya* meant.

'It depends,' answered the halfbreed. 'It can mean *The Yawner* or *The Talker*, mostly it means someone whose mouth stays open a lot.'

'He sure liked to talk,' grinned Cannon. 'Feller like that could talk a man to death.'

'He's got another name,' said Azul. 'Whitemen mostly call him Geronimo.'

'Jesus!' said Cannon, his own mouth opening in surprise. 'I didn't know.'

Azul went on grinning. 'Now you got another claim to fame. There's not too many whites get to sit around jawing with Geronimo.'

Cannon stayed silent, wondering if all the stories he

had heard about the infamous war-leader were true. Maybe not, he decided. Geronimo – Goklya – had seemed a likeable fellow. Maybe the stories got exaggerated the same way his own legend had built up. Or then again, maybe not.

'How come he's called Geronimo?' he asked after the shock had passed. 'I never heard him called Goklya before.'

'Goklya's his Apache name,' said Azul. 'The Mexicans gave him the other. Way I heard it, they named him after a saint. Saint Jerome. He liked to talk, too, so they nicknamed Goklya Jerónimo. That's Spanish for Jerome. Over the border the *J* got changed to a *G*.'

'You know him well?' Cannon asked. 'He knew you.'

'Some,' said the halfbreed. 'He rode with Mangas Colorado. Mangas was my grandfather, on my mother's side.'

'Christ!' Cannon shook his head, laughing. 'I guess I teamed up with someone famous. Maybe some day someone will write a book about us.'

'That'll be the day,' Azul smiled.

They reached the Gila west of the confluence with the San Francisco and began to follow the river west towards Fort Thomas. The country here was rugged, naked stone supplanting the timber of the southerly terrain, so that they rode down granite canyons with the river washing loud and fierce below them. Buzzards wheeled high above, black specks against the brilliant blue, drifting away to the west when it became obvious neither man was ready yet to provide the carrion-feeders with provenance.

Their path took them down a narrow trail flanked on one side by sheer walls of burnished rock, on the other by the precipitous drop down to the river. The air was cooler inside the deep stone canyons and once the sun was gone down behind the ridges there was a chill that bit deep. Azul noticed that Cannon got a little slower starting each morning, leaving his blanket with barely-concealed reluctance to crouch by the fire massaging his shoulders and legs. It was the first real sign the halfbreed had seen of the gunfighter's age, and he decided to wait over a spell in Fort Thomas to allow the older man some rest before starting on the next leg of their journey. He was not sure how far it was to Utah, certain only of the fact that the going would get nothing but harder. No longer sure of Cannon's endurance.

He felt a curious concern for the ageing gunfighter. A sympathy born of their shared wandering and that unvoiced kinship he had felt back in Valverde. In part it was to do with Cannon's growing respect for Indians, with his willingness to learn; in part to do with his toughness, his refusal to give in to the aches of age. So he slowed down himself, letting Cannon dictate the pace as they wound through the canyons to the open space dominated by the fort.

Fort Thomas was built close against the bank of the Gila, a dark, squat shape that dominated the grassland running out all around to wash green against the surrounding bulk of the ridges. The original military settlement had expanded into a full-blown township, stores and houses clustering about the protective ramparts. Look-out towers dominated the corners of the rectangular fortifications, a jetty running from the northern wall out into the river where a raft was moored. Troopers were visible in the towers, their dark blue shirts and yellow braces clear against the sky. The gates were open, exposing a Gatling gun that shone bright and lethal in the noonday sun.

Despite the number of civilian buildings around the fort, the majority of the men on the streets wore military blue. And the few women they saw were dressed in the gaudy fineries of whores, their painted eyes following the two men with calculating glances as they rode slowly towards the largest of the saloons. It was a two-storey place with a false front adding further height, a narrow balcony shading the door below. Above the door was a painted sign announcing the place as The Palace, and advertising rooms. Inside there was a preponderance of uniforms that outnumbered the civilians on a ratio of about three to one. A piano was tinkling at the far end of the plank-floored room, and the long bar was crowded with drinkers. After the clean air of the mountains, the atmosphere was fetid with the odour of unwashed bodies, thick with tobacco smoke.

They pushed up to the bar and Cannon called for whiskey. The barkeep set an open bottle in front of him, then added a single glass. He took Cannon's money and started to turn away.

'Two glasses,' said the gunfighter. 'You blind?'

The barkeep wiped a strand of pomaded hair from his forehead and stared at Cannon like he was looking at a sick horse.

'He ain't white, mister.'

'So?' Cannon demanded.

'So I don't serve likker to injuns or halfbreeds.' The barkeep shrugged. 'Military regulations.'

Azul's face tightened, his mouth flattening to a thin line. The barkeep saw the expression and shrugged again. 'Ain't my doin', feller. I had my way, I'd sell likker to anyone with the money to buy it. It's regulations.'

Cannon started to say something, but Azul shook his head, looking round at the uniforms surrounding them.

'Leave it, Abe.'

Cannon's own features had settled into a grim mask, but he nodded, recognising the sense in the halfbreed's warning.

'All right. We'll take the bottle with us. You got rooms?'

'Sure.' The barkeep nodded. 'I got rooms fer white-men. Yore friend can most likely find a place with the scouts. They got a barracks inside the fort.'

'Regulations?' queried Cannon.

'No likker to be sold to injuns or them as got injun blood. No likker to be sold to any whitemen fer the purpose o' supplyin' it to injuns or them as got injun blood.' The barkeep recited it by rote; like a child chanting a lesson in school. 'No rooms to be occupied by injuns or them as got injun blood. No injuns allowed in the eatin' room. Or them as got injun blood. Don't blame me, mister. You want to argue it, you go see Colonel Canfield. He's the one made the rules, an' I can't afford to break them.'

'Jesus!' Cannon's voice was still soft, but there was an edge to it now. 'We just rode a hundred odd miles through Apache country an' we can't get a drink.'

The argument had already attracted the attention of the soldiers closest to them. Now the gunfighter's last comment sparked a grunt of surprise from a big tow-headed sergeant. He was a tall man, a head over Azul's height, with the muscle of his belly turning soft above his belt. His face was red from whiskey and his small grey eyes got narrow and curious.

'You say you come through Apache country?'

Cannon looked at him. Glanced at the stripes on his sleeve. 'You hear real good, Sergeant.'

The man ignored the sarcasm. 'You come with me. The colonel's gonna want to talk to you.'

Cannon ignored him, turning back to the barkeep. 'Can we sleep in the stable? Or is that covered by regulations?'

The barkeep shook his head.

The sergeant said, 'I told you to come with me.'

Cannon said, 'Maybe you don't hear so good after all. We just come a long way an' now we're lookin' for some soft straw an' a bath. You tell the colonel we'll be around. He wants to talk, he can come find us.'

The sergeant's face shifted colour from red to purple. A band of freckles stood out across the bridge of his bulbous nose. He opened his mouth to speak again. Then closed it as Cannon's hand brushed the butt of the Peacemaker. Azul moved sideways to give Cannon room. His own right hand was close to his gun.

'He ain't armed,' warned the barkeep. 'That's regulations.'

The troopers with the sergeant formed a semi-circle facing the gunfighter and the halfbreed. Down the room the piano fell silent. More soldiers turned to watch.

Azul kept his gaze concentrated on the tow-head, his ears tuned to pick up any movement behind him. They were close enough to the door to get out fast if it came to a fight. Would need to: even though the off-duty troopers were not carrying guns there were too many to handle. And the civilians were armed; and moving up to join the soldiers.

Cannon, too, saw the impossibility of it and took a pace backwards.

'We'll be stabling our horses,' he said. 'Then we'll take a bath. Then we're gonna eat. After that, your colonel can come talk if he wants.'

There was something in his voice that told the sergeant he wouldn't live to see the finish of any fight he might start. He glowered at Cannon and Azul. Nodded reluctantly.

'I'll tell him that. Just like you said it. He ain't gonna like it. Nor do I. I'll remember you.'

'Yeah.' Cannon eased towards the door. Azul went with him, backing across the sidewalk to the hitching rail. Over the curved top of the batwings faces watched them.

They unhitched their mounts and walked the animals down the street towards the livery. Behind them boots thudded on the boards as the sergeant and a trooper ran in the direction of the fort.

'Welcome to civilisation,' murmured Azul. 'How's it feel to be back?'

Cannon spat in the dust.

* * *

The livery stable was cool and dark and quiet. The old man and the boy playing pinochle by the doors took a dollar each for the horses and fifty cents to let them sleep over in an empty stall. They bathed under the flow of water from a pump out back, drinking the whiskey Cannon had brought from the saloon. After cleaning up, they found a small eatery that didn't seem to be covered by military regulations where a fat woman in a strained calico dress gave them pork tenderloin with hash browns and a mess of greens. By the time they were finished it was late afternoon.

'Now what?' Cannon asked. 'Looks like we'll start a war if we try to get a drink.'

'You can,' Azul replied. 'Go ahead.'

'The hell I will.' Cannon grinned. 'I ain't leavin' you on your lonesome. No tellin' what trouble you'd start.'

Azul smiled: whatever doubts had existed seemed gone now.

'I'd thought to stop over,' he said, 'but that doesn't seem like a good idea anymore.'

'No,' Cannon agreed, 'it don't. Whyn't we get supplies? Then start early come morning?'

'Sure.' Azul nodded.

They went into a general store. Cannon purchased coffee and salt and flour; some dried beef and some salted pork; cartridges. They carried the stuff back to the stable.

And found a lieutenant waiting for them with five men. On duty: they were all wearing sidearms.

'Lieutenant Murray.' He touched his hat. 'Colonel Canfield requests your presence. Immediately.'

'That an invitation or an order?' Cannon asked.

'Sounds like an offer we can't refuse,' said Azul.

Murray smiled tightly. 'There's been trouble,' he said. 'Anyone coming from the south sees the colonel.'

'What trouble?' Azul asked.

Murray looked at him. He seemed to find it difficult deciding if he should answer a halfbreed. Then he shrugged, 'Apache trouble. Colonel Canfield will tell you. Follow me.' There was a slight pause before he added, 'Please.'

The troopers shifted position so that they formed a group around the two men. Their faces were mostly blank, but the youngest kept glancing curiously at Azul. Lieutenant Murray led the way out of the stable at a brisk march.

The sun was just beginning its descent to the western horizon and the air was very still, not yet cooling down. On the street people paused to watch the squad of Army men escorting Azul and Cannon towards the fort. The gates were still wide, the Gatling gun still shining. The American flag hung limp on its post at the centre of the parade ground. Smoke was lifting lazily from the chimney of the mess hall, and as they strode towards the neatly-painted command hut a squadron of cavalry went past at the trot. Lieutenant Murray halted at the foot of the steps leading up to the command post and snapped off a salute that was answered by the two men on guard.

'Lieutenant Murray to see Colonel Canfield with the two travellers.'

One of the guards executed a neat about-face and shouted through the open door. A gruff voice answered, shouting for them to come in.

Colonel Canfield was a direct contrast to Lieutenant Murray. Where the junior officer was slim, Canfield was fat. Where Murray's hair was thinning, Canfield's was thick, cropped to stubble shortness. Where Murray's uniform was neat, Canfield's was an ash-marked sack that strained over his belly. Murray stood to attention while his commanding officer slumped behind a wide mahogany desk with a big cigar in his mouth. His face was tanned and bland, clean-shaved in contrast to Murray's beard. Veins stood out red on his nose. His hands were unnaturally large, with coarse black hair curling over the backs. When he spoke his voice was harsh.

'Sergeant Fletcher says you was trying to buy the halfbreed likker.'

He addressed himself to Cannon.

Cannon stared at him, not answering.

'Well?' Canfield barked. 'What you got to say.'

'I got a voice of my own,' rasped Azul, irritation rising. 'I speak English.'

Canfield took the cigar out of his mouth. The movement dislodged ash that fell unnoticed down his tunic.

'You two better get something straight.' He looked at Azul now, anger flickering in his cold green eyes. 'This ain't no soft-belly civilian town. Fort Thomas is Army all the way down the line. The Army made this place an' the Army runs it. I'm in command here, an' that means I run the place. I make the rules an' I make up the punishments for any goddam stupid saddlebums try to break them. You understand that?'

'I get the idea,' murmured the halfbreed.

'You better,' grunted Canfield.

Lieutenant Murray cleared his throat, looking embarrassed.

'Well?' snapped the colonel.

'They were buying supplies, sir. Looking to be planning on leaving.'

'That right?' Canfield asked.

'Come morning,' said Cannon.

'You don't like Fort Thomas?'

'Don't seem that Fort Thomas likes us,' said the gunfighter. 'Too many regulations.'

Canfield snorted. 'What you got to say?' he asked Azul. 'In American.'

'We're passing through.' Azul kept his voice flat and calm. 'Headed for Utah.'

'I don't give a mule's fart where you're goin',' said the fat man. 'It's where you come from I'm interested in. What blood you got?'

'Chiricahua,' said Azul. 'And white.'

'I got Cherrycow scouts,' Canfield said. 'They're pretty good. For injuns.'

'You wanted to talk,' Cannon suggested. 'What about?'

'About injuns an' goddam injun traders,' grated the colonel. 'I got word that bastard Geronimo's up this way again. You see any sign of him?'

Azul held his face straight; expressionless. Cannon spoke first.

'No,' he said. 'Not a sign.'

'Where you come from?' Canfield stared hard at the gunfighter.

'Place called Valverde,' answered Cannon. 'Down to New Mexico.'

'Why you goin' to Utah?'

'I got some land there. Reckoned it was time I settled down.'

'What you do?' Canfield looked suspicious. 'By way of a living.'

'I been hiring out.' Cannon touched his pistol.

'Name?' Canfield blew smoke across the desk in a thick, pungent cloud.

'Abe Cannon.'

'Never heard of you. His?'

'Gunn,' said Azul. 'Matthew Gunn.'

'Christ!' Canfield chuckled. It was an ugly sound. 'I meant your real name.'

'I was christened in Santa Fe,' said the halfbreed. 'Gunn was my father's name.'

'Kieron Gunn?' asked Canfield. 'Santa Fe trader? Injun lover?'

Azul nodded.

'What the Cherrycows call you?'

'Azul,' he said. 'You knew my father?'

'Ole bastard beat the shit outta me one time,' grinned Canfield. 'On account o' something I said about injuns. Didn't change my mind none, though. Why you ridin' with him?'

Azul shrugged. 'Why not?'

'Mister.' Canfield put the cigar down. 'Don't get smart with me. I ask a question, you answer it. Unless you want to get whipped.'

'He's guiding me,' intervened Cannon. 'Through the Apache country.'

Canfield's eyes screwed up. 'A gunslick an' a halfbreed wanderin' all over hostile country? That don't sound likely.'

'They've come a long way,' Murray stepped in. 'I checked their horses. They're not carrying enough to trade.'

'Don't mean they haven't,' growled the fat man. 'Don't mean they won't.'

'Sir,' Murray began, but Canfield waved him to silence.

'Let them speak.'

'We wouldn't come here,' said Azul. 'That don't make sense. Not if we'd been selling guns. We wouldn't buy here, either.'

'No,' allowed Canfield, not liking to admit the logic. 'I guess not. Been some raids, though. Party of silver miners went missing a while back, an' there's a buck called Enjuh out on the prod. You come across him?'

Azul shook his head. Cannon said, 'Never heard of him.'

Canfield picked up his cigar and sucked smoke into his lungs. 'All right. I guess I have to take yore word. I got nothing to hold you on, so you can go. But you better be gone early.'

'Sure,' said Cannon. 'The sooner the better.'

'Sounds like you don't like our town,' grunted Canfield.

'No,' said Cannon. 'Not much.'

Canfield laughed. 'Get them outta here, Lieutenant. Make sure they're gone come sun-up.'

'Sir!' Murray snapped off a neat salute and motioned for Azul and Cannon to follow him out. Behind them they could hear the commanding officer muttering something about goddam halfbreeds and goddam West Point starch-shirts.

'Forthright kind of man,' murmured Cannon as they

crossed the parade ground again. 'Speaks his mind, don't he?'

'Apaches killed his wife,' said Murray. 'He's a good soldier for all he's hard on Indians.'

'And halfbreeds,' added Azul.

'Mexican halfbreeds sold the Apaches whiskey,' said Murray. 'Then guns. They got the Indians likkered up, then talked them into raiding a stage. Canfield's wife was on it. After that he turned sour.'

They reached the gates and Murray halted. The sky was darkening now, light only at the farthest edge of the western horizon. Lanterns were burning in the windows of the saloons. Over by the stock pens a mule brayed in rising crescendo.

'Listen,' said Murray. 'I'm maybe speaking out of turn, but Canfield meant exactly what he said. If you're not gone by sun-up, I'll have to ride you out of town.'

'Don't worry,' Azul replied. 'We'll be gone.'

Murray nodded, toying with the empty fastenings for his sabre.

'There's something else. Sergeant Fletcher. He hates Indians worse than the colonel. And Canfield turns a blind eye if Fletcher beats up on anyone like you.'

'We can look after ourselves,' said Cannon. 'Don't worry.'

'Maybe you don't understand,' said Murray. 'But you riled Fletcher today, so he's liable to come looking for you. You harm him and Canfield will have you in the stockade. Or worse.' He looked at Azul nervously. 'You, in particular.'

Azul nodded. 'I'll remember. Thanks.'

Murray shrugged. 'I have to obey my orders. I don't have to like them.'

He watched as they walked away down the street. He was frowning.

They went back to the fat woman's eating house and ordered dinner.

'How come you didn't tell him?' asked Azul.

'Tell him what?' Cannon sounded innocent.

'About Enjuh and Goklya,' murmured the halfbreed.

Cannon smiled. 'I never was too good with names. Guess I just forgot.'

'I thought you was called Honest Abe,' countered Azul. 'You just proved the whiteman speaks with forked tongue.'

'Hell,' grinned Cannon, 'that was just a little red lie.'

CHAPTER SEVEN

Sam Fletcher had been a sergeant for ten out of the twenty-five years he had spent in the Army. He might have made the promotion earlier, if it wasn't for his hair-trigger temper and his readiness to use his fists. Twice he had reached corporal, then got busted down to the ranks again. Once when he reduced a fellow non-com to a bloody pulp in a Silver City whorehouse, and once when the shave-tail mule he'd assigned a green trooper stomped all over the boy while Fletcher looked on laughing. He had made sergeant under Colonel Canfield's command: the officer recognised in Fletcher the same rage that possessed him, while Fletcher found in Canfield the kind of officer he could respect.

They had served together in Fort Stockton, Fort Quitman, Fort Stanton, Camp McDowell, Fort Apache and Camp Grant before the posting to Fort Thomas. Fletcher's entire experience of Army life had been spent either fighting Indians or waiting to fight them. He hated them. The same way he hated Negros and Chinamen: anyone who wasn't white. By Canfield's standards he was a good soldier, and in a fight he possessed the kind of furious bravery that brought him to the attention of his commanding officers and made the men below him dread assignment to his squad. They called him Canfield's Boy – but always behind his back.

Three times he had gotten into trouble with the civilian authorities for fighting off duty, and each time Canfield had gotten him off. In Fort Thomas he was in his element: Canfield was in command and Fletcher had a more-or-less free rein on his temper.

And now his temper was high. He had been faced

down by a goddam civilian and a stinking halfbreed. And in Fletcher's book a halfbreed was a step down from a full-blooded Indian, which made Azul less than human.

Fletcher had seen death looking at him in The Palace saloon, and he hadn't liked it. He wasn't afraid of it, but he wasn't about to throw his life away going up against a gunfighter and a murderous 'breed with eyes like blue ice and a Colt on his hip. When he had relayed his message to the colonel he had received the clear understanding that he was free to extract whatever revenge he thought fit. No questions asked. What Fletcher thought fit was that he take a few men with him and work the two over. Not kill them – that might be more than even Canfield could ignore – but rough them up enough they wouldn't be riding anywhere for a spell.

He chose his men carefully. Three troopers of much the same mind, all good at the kind of vicious in-fighting Fletcher enjoyed. The trouble was he didn't doubt that Cannon and the halfbreed wouldn't hesitate to use their guns, so he needed to catch them off guard. Which looked like he would have to wait until they were asleep. That was all right because it gave him time to sink a bottle in The Palace while the sun went down and the night got dark, and the whiskey served only to fuel the fires of his anger. He waited until the man he had posted to watch the stable brought word the two were bedding down for the night and then made his move.

The stable was closed up for the night. The straw in the empty stall was fresh, sweet-smelling. It mingled with the odour of the horses to produce a pleasant scent that induced a lazily sleepy feeling. If anything, the livery was probably more comfortable – and a deal cleaner – than the beds offered by The Palace. To whites. Azul watched as Cannon spread his blanket on the makeshift bed, then humped a pile of straw into a body-sized shape and draped his own blanket over the mound. In the dim light it looked like a sleeping body, the black stetson covering the face.

'What's that for?' Cannon stretched, yawning. 'Ain't you sleeping here?'

Azul shook his head. He pointed at the loft. 'I'll be up there.'

'You thinking about that sergeant?' Cannon grinned. 'He won't try anything.'

'Maybe, maybe not.' Azul shrugged. 'If he does we could be in trouble.'

'Canfield?' asked Cannon.

'We shoot him, we'll get hung.' Azul watched the gunfighter check his Colt. 'You heard what Murray said.'

Cannon went on grinning. 'I seen soldierboys like that before. Mostly they're all wind an' piss. We won't need to shoot him – just pull a gun. He'll back down.'

'I don't think so,' murmured the halfbreed. 'I think he'll push it through. And he won't come alone.'

'Yore choice.' Cannon dropped onto the straw with a grateful sigh. 'Me, I'm gonna forget him an' get me some sleep.'

Azul nodded and began to climb the ladder up to the loft. It ran around three sides of the livery, stacked with bales and sacks of grain. It was some fifteen feet above the floor, with a clear view of the doors and the stalls below. Azul made himself a bed close to the ladder and settled down, his gunbelt beside him on the hay. He closed his eyes and let himself drift into the light sleep he had learnt raiding with the Chiricahua. Undisturbed, it would afford him all the rest he needed; but a sound – a hint of danger – would lift him to instant wakefulness, ready to act.

And as he gave way to the drowsiness he remembered something his father had told him a long time ago, as they sat watching the sun go down over the Mogollons.

'I told you you're gonna meet trouble on account of your blood,' Kieron Gunn had said. *'You're gonna come across whitemen all eaten up with hate for anyone with Indian blood. You'll meet Indians who think the same*

way about the whites. It don't make sense, but that's just the way some folks are. You run up against that kind, you don't take no crud. Stand up for yourself. Show them you're just as good as them, but don't go looking for trouble. Especially not when you're around whites. Your mother's people, most of them don't give no never-mind what colour you are so long as you show yourself a man. Whites, though, they're different. Some Indian spits in your eye on account your father's white, you can settle it between you. The same thing happens in a town, you have to be careful. You fight a man in a town and you could wind up in jail. Or all them other God-fearin', law-abiding citizens might just decide to lynch you on account they don't think a man with Indian blood's got the right to lay hands on a white.'

'Why?' Azul had asked. *'Why should it be different?'*

And Kieron Gunn had shrugged and said, *'No reason. It just is. It's something called intolerance. When it happens you have to decide how you'll handle it. But remember that sometimes there's an old saying applies pretty good: discretion's the better part of valour.'*

Azul smiled sleepily, deciding that he had shown enough discretion that day. If Fletcher came looking for trouble he would find it.

Fletcher was ready. The first bottle had stoked his anger and now the second was lifting it past the boiling point. It passed from hand to hand as he led his men down the street. They carried no guns, but two of the troopers had picked up axe hafts and the third was carrying a switchblade. Fletcher scorned weapons, confident that his fists alone would be enough once they had disarmed the two men.

His plan was simple: give them time to get bedded down, then go in fast. Hit them in a rush and take the guns off them before they got a chance to use them. Then have some fun. Teach the bastards a lesson they wouldn't forget in a hurry.

The thought that Canfield had ordered them out of

town was icing on the cake of the sergeant's revenge. The way he had it worked out, neither man would be in any condition to ride by the time the sun rose, so they'd be flouting the colonel's direct order. Which would mean a spell in the stockade at the least, maybe a flogging. Fletcher liked that idea: he would be handling the whip.

He called a halt a few yards from the livery doors and drained the bottle. Set it down quietly. Then he flexed his big hands and nodded to his men. A trooper with a broken nose positioned himself before the man-size door set into the wider gates. On Fletcher's signal he booted the door inwards and followed the sergeant through in a fast run.

A horse snickered as the door crashed open. Lanterns were burning dimly at either end of the stable's aisle, their light augmented by the waning moon that was shining in through the windows set high up in the side walls. The air was dusty, a misty grey in the pale light. Fletcher blinked, adjusting his vision. All the stalls save one were occupied by horses. He pounded towards the empty stall.

And halted as the triple *click!* of Cannon's hammer going back reminded him he didn't have the full advantage. Yet.

The gunfighter was up on one elbow, the Peacemaker in his right hand with the muzzle pointed at the front of the stall. At Fletcher's spreading gut. His grey hair was mussed and little pieces of straw clung to his moustache. For an instant he looked his full age, but then the hard, cold light woke in his eyes and his voice caught its full authority.

'What the hell you want?'

'You,' snarled Fletcher. 'You an' the goddam halfbreed.'

Cannon smiled tensely. 'You don't get us, Sergeant. Back off.'

'You ain't gonna kill me.' Fletcher sneered, confident of his position. 'You ain't gonna chance that.'

'I don't have to kill you.' Cannon's voice was cold as the light in his eyes. 'I can put a bullet through your knee. Maybe someplace a bit higher.'

Fletcher shook his head. 'Not in Fort Thomas, feller. Not if you want to ride away.' He sniggered as he added, 'After I finished with you.'

One of the troopers, a skinny man called Greenock, said, 'The 'breed sure sleeps sound.'

Fletcher frowned. 'Maybe he's likkered up. Maybe this old man's been feedin' him whiskey. Against regulations.'

The men with him chuckled.

And a voice that was cold and flat and deadly said, 'No. I buy my own.'

Fletcher turned his head, squinting into the half-light.

'The loft, Sarge.' A man called Skinner pointed upwards. 'He's there.'

Fletcher craned his thick neck round and up. And saw the ugly black hole of a Winchester's muzzle staring back at him.

'You ain't gonna use that.'

'No?' grated Azul.

The way he said it left no doubt in the sergeant's mind. Suddenly the whiskey rage was blown away. It was replaced with a different kind of fury, a cooler, but more bitter anger at the frustration of his plans. He tried to bluff it out, not wanting to be faced down a second time.

'You'll hang. You pull that trigger an' you're a dead man.'

'You'll show me the way,' rasped Azul. 'You'll be there before me.'

A sour taste formed in Fletcher's throat. He spat, conscious of sweat trickling slow and cold down his back. Cannon climbed to his feet, grunting slightly as he straightened.

'Christ!' whispered Skinner. 'He means it.'

'Drop those clubs,' Azul ordered.

Skinner and Greenock let the axe hafts fall to the

floor. The third trooper, McIntyre, cupped his hand around the switchblade.

'Now move to the centre.' Azul came to the head of the ladder. 'Abe?'

'I got them covered.' Cannon came out of the stall with the Colt at waist height.

Azul held the rifle in his right hand as he descended the ladder. On the floor of the stable the moonlight shone on his face. It transformed the mane of sun-bleached hair to an almost-white colour. It emphasised the blue of his eyes. They were very cold, like ice on the bottom of a fresh-dug grave.

'All right,' he said, his tone matching the bleakness of his gaze. 'You figger you got some kind of quarrel with us. Spell it out.'

Fletcher stared back. Whatever else might be said about the man, he could not be accused of lacking courage.

'Goddam halfbreed,' was all he said.

'You don't like halfbreeds?' Azul's mouth was flattened to a thin line.

'Goddam squaw droppings,' grunted Fletcher. 'I'm gonna take you apart.'

McIntyre chose that moment to act. He let the switch-blade drop through his fingers, fastening his grip on the haft. His arm came up, tensing back for a throw. Then he screamed as the Winchester shifted slightly in Azul's hands and the muzzle spat flame.

The .44-40 slug hit the trooper in the wrist. It shattered the radius and ulna bones, tearing out the back on a spray of blood from the severed veins. McIntyre's fingers opened, the knife dropping to the floor. His hand flopped loose and he clutched at the wound with his left. His face was unnaturally pale, speckled with blood. His lips drew back from his grinding teeth and a harsh whimpering sound came out.

Fletcher roared an inarticulate cry and charged Cannon.

The gunfighter sidestepped, wary of chancing the consequences of killing a soldier. Instead, he dropped the Colt's hammer and thrust a foot into the sergeant's path, swinging the Peacemaker at the same time so that the barrel smashed against Fletcher's neck. The big man went down on all fours, shaking his head.

Azul crossed the distance separating him from Greenock and Skinner in two long strides. As he closed, he brought the Winchester up and round in a vicious arc that ended against the underside of Greenock's jaw. The skinny soldier's head snapped back, shards of broken enamel chipping from his teeth. Azul pivoted, bringing the barrel of the rifle down over Skinner's out-thrust arms. Skinner yelled and cannoned against him. Azul stepped back, lifting his right leg to drive the knee hard into the trooper's groin. A high-pitched shriek erupted from Skinner's open mouth and he went down in a foetal ball, his hands pressed tight around his manhood. Azul kicked him in the face. There was a squelchy sound and twin streamers of blood spilled from the man's nostrils, joining as they ran down his chest. His eyes crossed and then closed. His body twitched, urine staining the front of his faded blue pants.

Greenock was shaking his head. Spitting chunks of tooth onto the straw. His eyes were wide, radiating a mixture of fear and fury. They closed as the halfbreed drove the barrel of the Winchester into his belly. Greenock doubled over, his breath coming out in a long, moaning wheeze. Azul lifted the rifle and slammed the stock down against the man's back, just above the belt. The wheezing was instantly replaced with a gasp and Greenock went down on his face, body arcing back against the agony flooding his kidneys. Azul kicked him in the side, in the soft part between the ribs and the pelvic girdle. Greenock began to writhe, drawing his knees up tight against his chest then thrusting his legs out straight as though the movement would dispel the pain. Azul swung the rifle again, landing the stock against the side of the trooper's head. Beneath the surface of the skin blood vessels burst, a great red patch spreading over the man's face from the temple to the jawline. Blood pooled under his face, spilling from his mouth and ear, and he grunted then fell still and silent.

McIntyre was still clutching his shattered wrist, trying to stem the flow of blood. His features were ashen in the moonlight, his lips working in a soundless mumble. Azul hit him once at the base of the neck and he slumped forwards, stretching full length over the straw. His right hand stuck out at an angle to the arm. Sharp edges of bone jutted through the torn flesh, the white stained crimson. A growing pool began to form beneath the wound.

'Bastards!' Fletcher was on his knees now. 'Goddam bastards!'

Cannon holstered the Peacemaker. 'What about him?'

Fletcher stood up. 'You wouldn't have done it without guns. Bastards like you don't have the guts to face a man fair.'

'You call four on two fair?' snapped Cannon. 'That yore idea of fair?'

'Leave him,' said Azul; slow and ugly. 'It's me he wants.'

'An' I'll get you.' Fletcher rubbed at his neck, his face set in vicious lines. 'You got my word on that.'

Azul tossed the Winchester to Cannon.

'You got your chance right now.'

Fletcher stared at him. Then at Cannon. The gunfighter shrugged. Fletcher looked back at Azul. Deep inside his small grey eyes the light of an idea burned. His head thrust forwards, his shoulders bunching as his hands closed into fists. He looked like a bull getting ready to charge. Azul braced his legs, left foot extended slightly forwards, hands dangling loose by his sides.

'You want it?' he taunted. 'You got the guts?'

Fletcher growled deep in his throat and charged at the halfbreed, his huge fists windmilling air.

Azul moved only slightly. Just enough to shift his body out of the soldier's path. His arms came up, hands fastening on Fletcher's right wrist as his left leg went out to block the sergeant's way. He used Fletcher's own bulk, his own momentum, against the man so that as his leg tripped him he swung Fletcher forwards and round.

The soldier hurtled through the dim air. He sprawled full-length, sliding over the floor to crash against a stall. The horse inside whinnied and began to kick. Fletcher pushed up, cursing. He got back on his feet and charged in again, this time with arms spread wide, thick fingers reaching for Azul's throat. The halfbreed let him come. Let the clutching hands get close before he turned, his knees bending as he took hold of both wrists and leant forwards. Fletcher was lifted into the air. For an instant he was draped over Azul's back. Then he was somersaulting, shouting in surprise as he turned, the world spinning, to thud down close by the unconscious Greenock.

Azul stood calm, waiting. His face was impassive: cold and confident, not showing the anger he felt. He watched Fletcher roll onto his face and push upright again. Watched the big man come in slower this time, circling, seeking an opening. Fletcher's face was purple in the gloom, his breath coming in short, harsh gusts that blew whiskey fumes before him. Azul stood half-crouched, his own hands thrust out ready to grip and throw again. Then Fletcher feinted a move to the right, following it fast with a haymaker punch that could have flattened the halfbreed had it landed. But Azul was ducking under the blow, driving his own fist out to sink into the softening muscle above the soldier's belt.

Fletcher grunted, taking the blow. Taking the one that followed as he pounded a fist against Azul's face. The halfbreed grunted, feeling fire spread over his cheek, lights dance over his eyes. Fletcher hit him again, lighter this time as he was moving back, but still hard enough to send pain lancing through his chest.

Not that way, Azul decided. Not a stand-up fight. That way – fists against fists – the bigger man would win. Not through skill, but through sheer power. That and the blind, bull-like rage that possessed him. He moved back, shaking his head to clear it of the effects of the sergeant's punches. And Fletcher thought he saw an advantage. This was the kind of fighting he knew and loved: brute strength and bar-room tricks. Go in fast and hard and take what the other man could do before he was overwhelmed by Fletcher's strength. He grinned and swung a leg up in a savage kick.

Azul bent forwards, angling his body over the kick so that Fletcher's boot landed flat against the hard muscle of his stomach. He grabbed hold of the ankle, twisting it and pulling back. Fletcher shouted again as he felt his balance going. For an instant he tottered on one foot, and then he was spinning sideways to crash down for the third time.

He came up shaking his head, aware that he lacked the staying power for this kind of crazy injun fighting. Knowing that he needed to get his wind or end it fast. He began to circle again.

And the halfbreed smiled. It was an unpleasant expression that had nothing to do with humour.

'No guns,' he rasped. 'Just you and me. A fair fight.'

Fletcher snarled and came in with his head down. Azul braced himself, sucking in his belly; hardening the muscles there. He lifted both arms high above his head, fingers interlocking. As Fletcher's bull-charge struck he brought his left knee up at the same time as his arms came down. The elbows rammed against Fletcher's back as the knee connected with the soldier's face. The lips mangled on breaking teeth. Fletcher gasped, spitting blood. His vision went dark and only brute power kept him moving. Closed his arms around Azul's waist and carried the halfbreed backwards. Azul slammed a knee into the man's groin, surprised that he could withstand the force of the double blow. More surprised that he was still moving. He felt the slats of a stall ram against his back and then grunted as Fletcher drove his head forwards against his face. The sergeant's forehead was like scoured stone. It slammed against the bridge of Azul's nose. Came close to breaking bone.

Fletcher shifted his grip, grasping the woodwork of the stall so that his bulk held Azul pinned, crushing him between the stall and the sergeant's body. The horse began to scream, pounding its hooves against the wood. Fletcher grinned, blowing streamers of bloody mucus from his nostrils. He tightened his grip, twisting his head as he sought to fasten his teeth in Azul's neck.

Azul saw Cannon closing in with the Winchester lifted to club Fletcher. He grunted 'No!' and raised his legs, curving them around Fletcher's. The soldier felt the movement and brought a knee up in an attempt to kick the halfbreed. It was the reaction Azul had anticipated. The movement gave him the opening he wanted, allowing him to hook both legs behind Fletcher's knees. He locked his feet together, pulling the soldier in closer. Too late, Fletcher realised what was happening. He tried to straighten his legs, but instead felt them pulled forwards, bending involuntarily. He began to slide down Azul's body, forced to release the pressure against the halfbreed's chest as he grabbed the rails for support.

Azul felt his own legs descend and released his grip. He folded his arms against his chest and then brought them up together, inside Fletcher's hold so that the man's arms were forced apart. As his moccasins touched the floor he brought his lifted arms down together, slamming the edges of his hands hard against Fletcher's neck. The sergeant groaned as the double blow thudded onto the nerve centres. His eyes glazed and he let go the stall, staggering back.

He was still moving as Azul landed a foot against his right knee, toppling him. As he went down Azul landed a kick in the centre of his belly. Air blasted from Fletcher's lungs. He doubled up, rolling in anticipation of a second kick. None came and he climbed groggily to his feet, glaring through reddened, porcine eyes at the halfbreed.

Azul moved in again, taking the advantage before Fletcher's head cleared. He faked a kick and as the soldier twisted to avoid it, locked his fingers in the man's shirt. He hauled back, lifting his right foot to plant it hard against Fletcher's gut as he let himself go over backwards, balanced on his left foot. Fletcher was lifted into the air again, pivoting on the outthrust moccasin. Azul felt the floor against his back and let go Fletcher's shirt as he drove his leg straight. Fletcher's body described an arc through the air. He slammed face-first against the stall. Splinters lanced into his skin and as he fell to the ground, he felt the wood rasp against his face, tearing him. Azul rolled to his feet, grabbing a handful of tow-coloured hair. He dragged Fletcher's head back then rammed it forwards, smashing it viciously against the slats. Teeth spat from the sergeant's mouth. His eyes got hidden behind a curtain of blood. His nose pulped. And he went slack.

Azul let him go. Watching as he folded onto the floor; unconscious, bloody.

'We best get moving,' said Cannon. 'Canfield ain't gonna like this.'

Azul nodded, glancing round at the broken soldiers.

'They just don't make it,' he grinned. 'Not as Indian fighters.'

CHAPTER EIGHT

'Sir!' Lieutenant Murray stood to rigid attention. 'Is that wise?'

Colonel Canfield took a cigar from the humidor on his big mahogany desk. His fleshy fingers rolled the thing with surprising delicacy. He picked up a silver cutter and clipped the end neatly. Struck a match and turned the end of the cigar in the flame. Satisfied, he put the cigar in his mouth and applied the match to the tip. The cigar glowed red. Smoke eased lazily from Canfield's mouth. At last he looked up at Murray.

'You questionin' my orders, Lieutenant?'

Murray shook his head. 'No, Sir. I'm just . . .'

'Lieutenant!' Canfield cut him short: he was enjoying Murray's discomfort. 'I've got three troopers confined to sick quarters. One's got a busted nose an' a broken jaw. One's got busted ribs an' the doc says he's ripped up inside. The third is gonna lose his right hand. My best sergeant's got a face looks like a mule team stomped all over him. The doc reckons he could lose an eye. You approve of that, Lieutenant?'

'No, Sir.' Murray cleared his throat. He could feel his shirt getting sticky across his shoulders. 'But it was Sergeant Fletcher started it, Sir.'

Canfield's green eyes got very pale. 'Lieutenant,' he said slowly, almost softly: a bad sign. 'I don't give a fuck who started it. All I know is some goddam halfbreed an' a fucking no-account gunfighter rode into my town an' crippled four of my men. They are not going to get away with it. You are goin' to see to that, Lieutenant. You are goin' after them. You are goin' to find them an' bring them back. Alive, Lieutenant. So I can punish them.'

'They could be anywhere, Sir,' protested Murray. 'They left during the night, so they've got a head start.'

Ash fell from the colonel's cigar, tumbling unnoticed down his shirtfront.

'Lieutenant, you got your orders.'

Murray made one final try. 'Sir, with Geronimo reported in the area and Enjuh making trouble, is it wise to deplete the command?'

Canfield's face got red. 'They make you deaf at West Point, Lieutenant?'

'No, Sir!'

'Then you heard your orders?'

'Yes, Sir!'

'Then obey them, Lieutenant. Else I'll break you to the ranks an' you'll spend the rest of your term shovellin' shit in the stables.'

'Sir!' Murray snapped off a salute.

'And Lieutenant.' Murray paused at the door. 'You fail to bring them back, you better have some damn' good reasons.'

'Sir!'

Murray stepped out into the sunlight. It was a bright day. The Gatling gun shone in the brilliance. The square of grass around the flagpole looked very green. The flag fluttered in the slight breeze. From across the parade ground an elderly man in a white coat with major's insignia stitched to the shoulders beckoned to Murray. The lieutenant went over to him with a worried expression on his bearded face.

'Well?' asked the doctor. 'What's the verdict?'

'I have to find them,' said Murray. 'Find them and bring them back. Alive.'

'What we expected.' The medical officer shrugged. 'Canfield's Boy.'

'Canfield's Boy,' nodded Murray. 'How is he?'

'Bad,' said the doctor, not showing much concern. 'He lost most of his teeth. His jaw's bust in three places and he's got wood splinters lodged in one eye. He could lose it. McIntyre will lose the hand. He almost bled to death.'

'They asked for it,' said Murray. 'They got what they asked for.'

'You know that,' shrugged the major. 'I know that. It's still Canfield's Boy. And Canfield's still the commanding officer.'

'Yes,' said Murray. 'And I have my orders.'

'What will you do?' asked the major.

Murray shrugged, 'Ours not to reason why.'

'What?'

'Nothing.' The lieutenant turned away.

He crossed the parade ground to the barracks. Shouted orders. Twenty minutes later a squadron of cavalry was formed in line of twos. At the centre of the column a pair of mules carried field provisions. At the head, Murray conferred briefly with two Apache scouts. Canfield watched as they rode out through the gates. Murray could feel his eyes burning into his neck.

Azul slowed the pace as the sun climbed higher across the sky. They were over the ridge flanking Fort Thomas to the north and ahead of them the terrain stretched out in broken folds to the distant bulk of the Colorado Plateau. They had made good time, pushing both horses to their limits as they put hours between them and the fort. Between them and Canfield's wrath.

'Jesus!' Cannon stretched in the saddle, flexing his shoulders. 'They surely ain't gonna come this far after us.'

'You sound like an Indian.' Azul studied the ground ahead.

'How's that?' asked Cannon.

'Indians mostly fight until they've had enough,' said the halfbreed, 'then they stop. They run the same way: until they've had enough of running. Then they turn and fight.'

'Sounds sensible to me,' grunted the older man.

Azul grinned. 'I met a man once. He was looking for

a girl. A child, got taken by Comanches. He said they didn't know there was such a crittur as just kept on coming.'

'He find her?' Cannon asked. 'In the end?'

'I don't know,' said Azul. 'But he went on looking.'

'So?' queried Cannon.

'So I think maybe Canfield's like that,' said the half-breed. 'He'll go on looking.'

'And we go on runnin',' murmured the gunfighter. 'Shit!'

'Yeah.' Azul steered the grey horse down a slope dangerous with shale. A stream ran along the foot and he turned into it, heading eastwards, climbing out when a stretch of smooth rock presented a place where tracks wouldn't show. They climbed the rock and cut down off the hogback atop, traversing a tree-lined slope that bled out into a wooded valley. It wasn't the soldiers he felt certain Canfield would send after them that worried him. He was confident of losing any *pinda-lick-oyi* trailing him. But Canfield had Apache scouts in his command, and they could sniff out his path better than a hunting dog. And he didn't want to chance a fight: beating up four soldiers was something that would blow over in time, killing men wearing the uniform of the United States Army was something else.

'How long do we keep this up?' asked Cannon as they rested after manhandling the horses up a slope too steep to ride.

'As long as we need,' said Azul. 'Until I'm sure.'

The gunfighter nodded and lay back against the sun-warmed stone. He was breathing heavily, his face paled by the exertion, emphasising the creases so that they stood like knife cuts against the tan. Alone, Azul knew that he could outrun any pursuit. Could lose himself in the wilderness of the northern Arizona territory, even with Apache scouts hunting him. With Cannon there was a problem. The old man was unused to this kind of travelling and it was starting to show. He wasn't about to admit it, but Azul could see it in the set of his shoulders, in the way he climbed wearily from the saddle each time they halted. With Cannon it was going to be harder.

'All right.' He got to his feet. 'Let's go.'

Cannon sighed and climbed stiffly into the saddle, wincing as he settled onto the leather. Azul led the way along the ridge, cutting down through a stand of timber to swing north again along a steep-walled ravine. A narrow trail wound upwards at the farther end, devolving on yet another ridge that twisted away into a wasteland of jumbled rock and dense timber. The sun was up high now, burning out of a clear azure sky, reflecting off the stone in shimmering patterns of multi-coloured light that danced and shimmied before them. Azul held the grey stallion to an easy canter, as much to preserve its strength as to allow Cannon some rest. He didn't want to exhaust the gunfighter or the animals: all might need reserves of strength and speed if it came to a straight chase.

Lieutenant Murray took the tin plate his sergeant offered him with a grunt of thanks. The non-com was twice his age, a weather-beaten man with grizzled hair and a long scar down the right side of his face where an Apache knife had pared flesh to the bone. He brought his own food over and hunkered down facing the officer.

'Bavispe reckons they're a good half day in front, Sir.'

Murray nodded. 'They got good mounts, Landon. I saw them.'

Sergeant Landon spat a chunk of gristle into the fire. 'That's what's strange, Lieutenant. Bavispe says they ain't movin' so fast as they might.'

'He know why?' asked Murray.

'Nossir. Neither animal's lame an' they ain't packin' any real load. Bavispe reckons they could outrun us if they wanted. He says he's heard of the 'breed an' he thinks he could lose us if he wanted.'

Murray fidgeted a piece of fat from between his teeth and tossed it away. He looked at the sergeant, wondering what was going on inside the man's head. Landon was a thirty-year man with a deal more experience than his superior officer. Murray valued his opinion.

'You got any thoughts on that, Sergeant?'

Landon shrugged. 'I talked it over with Bavispe an' Julio. They reckon one of them could be hurt. That could be slowin' them.'

'No.' Murray stared into the fire. 'Best I could make out, it was Fletcher and his men took the hurts. Not the other two. The one called Azul – or Gunn – is part Chiricahua. He wouldn't slow if he was hurt. Turn and fight, maybe. But not slow.'

'How about the other?' asked Landon. 'The gunfighter.'

'Cannon?' Murray looked thoughtful. 'He was tough. Looked like he could handle himself. But he was old. Maybe that's slowing them.'

'Slowin' the halfbreed?' Landon sounded doubtful. 'That were so, wouldn't he leave Cannon?'

'No.' Murray shook his head. 'I don't think so. I don't think he'd leave Cannon.'

'Be a halfbreed's way,' opined the sergeant. 'The Apache blood showin' through.'

'You don't rate the Apache much?' asked Murray.

'Ain't a question of ratin' them,' grunted Landon. 'More like understandin' them. An Apache can fight like a cornered she-wolf when he wants. He can be the bravest goddam thing on God's own green world, but he's got his own way of doin' things. Ridin' herd on an old whiteman ain't one of them.'

'This one's different,' said Murray. 'I spoke with him, and he's not an ordinary man. If he's going slow, then he's got his own good reasons.'

'Sounds like you got respect for him,' suggested Landon. 'Beggin' yore pardon, Sir.'

Murray smiled wearily. 'No need to apologise, Sergeant.

You're right, anyway : I do have respect.'

'Maybe he's fixin' to bushwhack us. Slow us down.' Landon wiped a hunk of hard Army cornbread around his plate. 'Could be he's leadin' us into something.'

'Maybe.' Murray drank coffee. It was bitter. 'But if that were so, why didn't he kill Fletcher and the others? That would have made sense. Fletcher started this whole damn' thing.'

Landon sniffed, not speaking. Murray watched him for a while, a question forming in his mind that he wasn't sure he should ask. The hardline traditions of West Point military training didn't cover what was on his mind. But three years duty in Frontier forts had taught him that West Point traditions didn't always apply out here. Out here experience was what counted : a man with experience had to have lived long enough to gain it. And that made Sergeant Landon's opinion worth listening to.

'What do you think of this mission, Sergeant?' he asked at last. 'Speak your mind – it's off the record.'

Landon swilled coffee around his mug and took a deep breath.

'You really want that, Sir?'

Murray nodded.

'I think it's crazy,' said Landon. 'Fletcher an' them others are lucky they've lasted this long. They been askin' for a good stompin' a long time. Now they got it an' there ain't no one sheddin' no tears for them. They got what was comin', an' if it was the halfbreed an' the gunfighter done it, then I say good luck to them.'

'You don't think we should be chasing them?' murmured Murray.

'On account of Canfield's Boy?' Landon stared at the lieutenant. 'No, Sir, I don't. We got enough to worry about with Geronimo maybe in the area. I don't think we should be chasin' two men did what a whole lot of others have thought about.'

Murray nodded again, wondering if he had let the conversation go too far.

'It makes no difference, though. We still have orders.'

'Yessir!' Landon dropped his mug onto his plate. 'I was just venturin' an opinion.'

'Sure,' said the lieutenant. 'Like I asked you to. I guess we just do our best. Where are the scouts now?'

'Bavispe's gettin' hisself fed. I sent Julio out to take a look around.'

'Fine.' Murray stood up. 'Guess that's all we can do. Wake me if he reports anything.'

'Yessir!' Landon watched the young officer walk over to his bedroll. He had a lot to learn, but he was a decent man. As good an officer as any; better than some the sergeant could think of. Maybe he'd decide to do the sensible thing and just hike around a spell until the supplies ran down, then head back to the fort. He'd need to do some explaining to Canfield, but that would blow over: not even old Brassbelly could hold him responsible for losing a halfbreed in this godforsaken wilderness.

The sergeant spat into the fire and went to check the picket lines.

Azul chewed on the rabbit he had brought down, watching Cannon. So far the old man was holding up well, but that might not – most likely wouldn't – last. This kind of running and hiding wasn't what the gunfighter was used to, and the effects were showing at the end of the day worse than earlier. Cannon had admitted his stiffness when they halted for the night, and when Azul had returned with two rabbits over his shoulder Cannon hadn't heard him coming until he was in easy knife range. The start they had on any pursuit Canfield might have sent out could be whittled down, could be pared finer the next day. They were breaking trail – and the ground ahead was harder than any they had so far encountered – so if the Army was using Apache scouts they could be making faster time. Could ultimately catch up. Azul mulled it over and reached a decision.

And Cannon seemed to catch his thoughts.

'I'm slowin' you,' he said. 'You'd be long gone without me.'

'You sided me back in Fort Thomas,' murmured the halfbreed. 'I'll not quit you now.'

'They'll catch us up,' said Cannon. 'Leave me.'

'No.' Azul shook his head. 'I gave you my word. I'll see it through.'

He took the Bowie knife from its sheath and began to polish the heavy blade until it shone with a mirror brightness. Cannon watched him curiously.

'You got somethin' in mind?'

'Yeah.' Azul nodded. 'I just had a bright idea.'

CHAPTER NINE

Julio topped the rise and reined in, waiting for Bavispe to join him. He pointed at a section of rock where shod hooves had scraped the stone, then along the flank of the ridge to where the trees descended into the gully below. To untrained eyes the faint marks on the rock might have looked natural. To the two Chiricahua scouts they were like markers pointing the way.

Farther down the slope a twist of cotton dangled from a branch, and when Julio dismounted to lay his head on the ground he could see the loam under the trees indented the way a horse's hooves would push the spongey material down. Bavispe nodded and moved into the leader position. He came out of the trees where a stream ran down the centre of the gulley. There were no signs on the opposite bank, so he turned northwards: that was the general direction their quarry was taking. Had been taking for the past three days.

And each day the two Chiricahua sensed they were getting closer. The one called Azul was moving slower than he need, almost as though he wished them to catch up. It made them ride more carefully, not sure of his purpose. They had heard of the halfbreed. Knew he was wild as any *bronco*; a grandson of the great Mangas; and that made them wary. Whatever reason he had for letting them gain on him, they didn't want to ride into an ambush.

They were to Murray's squadron like the eyes in a man's head, and one good way to lose a tracker was to blind him. So they, in turn, had slowed and the chase was dragging out. So far the Lieutenant hadn't said anything about the slowing down, and the scouts guessed the *pinda-*

lick-oyi officer had as little stomach for it as they. But he had received his orders from Canfield himself, and they knew *el coronel* expected his orders to be obeyed. Even at the cost of lives.

So they pushed on. Warily. Cautiously. Riding with their Army-issue Springfields canted across their Army-issue saddles and their dark Apache eyes scanning each minute patch of ground ahead. Each place the one called Azul might lay in wait.

Higher up the stream Julio grunted and turned onto the bank. There were tracks leading off into the rocks, clear on the damp soil. They led into the rocks: a good place for an ambush.

Julio dismounted, motioning for Bavispe to follow suit. They stared up at the forbidding shapes, shadow-dark even in the afternoon sun. Nervously, the two Chiricahua studied the approach.

And something glinted. Something bright that flickered over their faces and sent them a message. They lowered their carbines and peered up at the jumbled stone, no longer afraid. Then the flickering came again and Bavispe lifted his Springfield high above his head in acknowledgement. The glinting ceased. Both scouts swung astride their ponies and rode – no longer wary – into the maze of rock.

Azul sheathed the Bowie and turned to Cannon.

'If this doesn't work we'll have to kill them.'

The gunfighter nodded and faded back into the mouth of a narrow cut. His Winchester was in his hands, a shell in the breech and the hammer back. He flattened behind a boulder, the rifle angled at the clearing in the stone where Azul stood waiting.

After a while a dark head came into view. Then a second. The two scouts halted, staring at the halfbreed. Azul waved them on with empty hands.

Bavispe said, 'You sent the shining. We come in peace.'

'You hunt me.' Azul motioned for them to dismount. 'You trail a brother like dogs.'

Julio shrugged and said, 'We take the *pinda-lick-oyi* soldier's pay. We are scouts.' He glanced round. 'Where is the other?'

'Watching,' said Azul. 'The ones you guide?'

Julio jutted a thumb over his shoulder. 'Half a day back. What is it you wish to talk about?'

Azul settled onto his haunches, clearing Cannon's field of fire. What came next would depend on the loyalty of the two Apache scouts, tribal blood against the promises made when they took scouts' pay.

'Why do you hunt us?' he asked.

'We were told to,' said Bavispe. 'It is our duty.'

'Why were you told to?' countered the halfbreed.

Bavispe frowned. 'You fought with the one called Fletcher.' He pronounced it *Flesh-hah*. 'You put him and the others in the *pinda-lick-oyi* medicine place. They are very badly hurt.'

Julio chuckled.

'And you would avenge Fletcher?' Azul questioned. 'You do this for him?'

Bavispe shook his head, suddenly confused. Julio said, 'What you did was a very good thing. The one called Fletcher was a pig. He beat me once and I would have killed him, but then I should have died with the *pinda-lick-oyi* rope around my neck, so I let him live. But I think that what you did to him is maybe better than killing him. Now everyone knows it was one of Cho-kon-en blood who did that to his face. I saw it through the window of the medicine place and it was very bad.'

Bavispe nodded, smiling at the memory.

'Then why hunt us?' asked Azul.

'We take the whiteman's pay,' said Julio. 'We have a duty.'

'To the *pinda-lick-oyi*?' asked Azul. 'Or to one whose mother was daughter of Mangas Colorado?'

Now Julio frowned. Bavispe began to chew on his lower lip. Neither man met the halfbreed's clear blue gaze.

'You think that what I did was right?' Azul said, letting

the words sink in before he added, 'Fletcher hates those of Apache blood.'

'This is known,' said Julio thoughtfully. 'Yes: I think you acted with honour. It is well you did it.'

Bavispe nodded.

'Then let us go,' said Azul. 'Brother to brother. The Apache way.'

It was the moment of crisis. The point of decision for the two scouts. Now would tell whether their loyalty rested with their own people or was given wholly to the Army. Now would decide whether or not they quit the rocks alive. They sensed this and looked first at one another, then at Azul.

Finally Julio said, 'We must talk about this between ourselves. It is not an easy thing to decide.'

'No,' agreed Azul, 'it is not. You are warriors. Men of honour. But now you must decide where the most honour rests.'

He stood up, walking away to the far side of the rocky clearing. The side opposite Cannon's position: that way the scouts would be caught in a crossfire. If it came to that. He hoped it wouldn't: he had no real desire to kill the two Chiricahua. But nor could he let them live if they refused his suggestion. Without them to guide the cavalry he could easily lose the squadron, even slowed by Cannon.

Time passed. The Chiricahua muttered softly, neither man raising his voice loud enough for the halfbreed to hear what they were saying. The sun shifted across the sky and the horses stood patiently, flicking their tails at the flies clustering about their flanks. One insect crawled unnoticed over Azul's face.

At last the two scouts nodded. Julio said, '*Enjuh,*' in a louder voice.

Azul moved to join them.

'We have decided,' said Julio, and Bavispe grunted his agreement. 'What you did was right. To punish you for that is wrong. You are of the blood and we shall let you go.'

'Thank you,' said Azul. 'What will you tell the soldiers?'

'That we have lost you,' said Julio. 'We shall lead them around for a few days more as if we truly hunted you. They will not know the difference, and in a while we shall tell Lieutenant Murray we have lost the trail. I do not think he will mind. I do not think he likes this much better than we.'

Bavispe nodded and said, 'I heard him talking with the one called Landon. The sergeant. I do not think either of them likes this. I know they do not like Fletcher.'

'It is good.' Azul nodded solemnly. 'I thank you for this.'

'You have our word on it,' smiled Julio. 'Now you can tell the old one to come out.'

Azul grinned and shouted for Cannon to show himself. The grey-haired man came out from the cut. He had the sense to hold his Winchester across his chest, not pointing at anyone.

'What would you have done if we had refused?' Julio asked.

Azul went on grinning as he said, 'Killed you. What else?'

Julio laughed. 'The *pinda-lick-oyi* named you well when they called you Breed. *Lobo*. Like a wolf.'

'A wolf knows his friends,' Azul replied. 'Go in peace, brothers.'

'May *Usen* guide your way,' said Bavispe. 'It is a hard trail you ride.'

Azul watched as they mounted their ponies and rode back down the slope. Without looking behind them they crossed the stream and got lost amongst the timber. They took their time rejoining the patrol, so that it looked like they had spent the full day hunting trail.

When Sergeant Landon questioned them, they told him the tracks were getting harder to follow over the stony ground. That the two horses had picked up speed and the quarry seemed to be drawing ahead, making up for lost time.

Landon reported this to Lieutenant Murray, who seemed relatively unconcerned.

'We'll continue come morning,' he decided. 'If we don't come up on them inside the week we'll turn back.'

'Yessir.' Landon wondered what had happened that day. There was something not quite right about the scouts' report. Nothing he could put a finger on, just a vague feeling. What the hell? he decided. He'd got no quarrel with the halfbreed, and the Lieutenant wasn't in any hurry to catch the man and bring him back like some goddam trophy for Canfield and his Boy to crow over. So where was the loss? Except to Canfield's pride. And Fletcher's sense of outrage.

The sergeant chuckled at the thought of Canfield's frustration. Then laughed out loud at the thought of Fletcher sucking broth through a straw.

'Something funny?' asked Murray. 'Want to share it?'

'Just thinking about Fletcher, Sir,' grinned the non-com. 'If we lose them he'll be real upset. Fit to bust a gut. He won't like it at all.'

'He'll just have to lump it,' grunted Murray. 'He'll have to swallow his pride.'

'He's having trouble swallowing right now,' murmured Landon. 'An' he's already got the lumps to prove it.'

Lieutenant Murray stared at his sergeant. Then he smiled and began to laugh.

Up on the ridge Azul was roasting a haunch of deer meat. Cannon was watching, letting the heat still retained by the rocks ease his aching back.

'What you say to them?' he asked.

Azul explained.

'An' they agreed?' Cannon grinned. 'They ain't chasin' us no more?'

Azul shook his head. 'No. It just goes to show.'

'What?' asked Cannon curiously.

Azul kept a straight face, 'Dead Indians aren't the only good ones.'

CHAPTER TEN

Azul and Cannon moved steadily northwards, following as direct a line as the country allowed. No longer forced to hide their tracks, they made better time, crossing the headwaters of the Salt west of Fort Apache where the land was high and rough and lonely. For fear Canfield might have sent gallopers ahead of them they avoided what few white settlements dotted the area. And whatever messages Enjuh or Gerónimo had sent on afforded them free passage through the northern boundaries of the Apache country.

Their way was lonely. Even the *rancherias* of the White Mountain tribes were thin on the ground up here, where eagles wheeled high above them and wolves howled in the night. Twice they passed under the distant gaze of watchful Indians, the mirror messages flashing between them and Azul in declaration of their right to cross the territory of the wild tribes. They followed the Cibicu Creek to its start high up in the mountains, traversing the rocky edge of the Great Divide to pick up the Chevelon Fork and steer along it to the confluence with the Little Colorado. The land flattened here, naked stone and wooded slopes giving way to high plains thick with wind-washed summer grass that ended where the Painted Desert began.

By now they were clear of Azul's homeground and he chose their way by guidance of the stars and the sun and the rivers. They followed the Little Colorado around the perimeter of the Painted Desert then cut north again to avoid the barrier of the Grand Canyon, picking up the mother river – the Colorado – north and east of the canyon. Somewhere along the way they crossed the invisible line dividing Arizona from the Utah territory. It was a meaningless division, existing only on the maps drawn up by white cartographers in the endless need of the *pinda-lick-oyi* to parcel up the land. To mark it off into sections that would show neatly on paper so that they might say 'Arizona ends here. Now it is Utah. Over there is New Mexico. There is California.' The real divisions were those set there by *Usen*, who made the mountains and the waters and the valleys that were the real boundaries. They were not even aware they had crossed the line until they came to a town that had a weathered board a quarter mile out from its single dusty street.

The board was cracked and faded, only the paint on it fresh. It carried a legend that read: *Welcome to Connaught. First town in Utah.*

The place was small. A run-down livery stable stood at one end of the street, a collapsed Mission building at the other. In between there was a dry goods store with yellow glass in the windows, a saloon with no windows, a hardware store and a scatter of houses. Nothing stood higher than a single storey and the buildings had about them an ageless look, bleached by the sun and scoured by the wind. Off to the west there was a graveyard surrounded by a dilapidated picket fence, more markers fallen down than were standing up.

They rode down the street to the livery. Handed over fifty cents that bought both horses a stall, fodder, and a rub-down. Cannon asked if they could get a hot bath.

The old man who took their money sniffed and chuckled. 'They got a bath over to the saloon, mister. Guess they can heat water if'n you're willin' to pay.'

They went over to the saloon. It didn't have any name and smelled worse than the old man. It was empty, save for a barkeep idly turning cards on a counter made up of rough-cut wood and used barrels. The floor was planked, creaking in protest as they crossed it and sending up little clouds of dust. The walls were wooden, chinked with clay and hung with slabs of cured meat. The meat was covered with flies.

The barkeep looked up as they approached, setting three glasses on the counter and producing an unmarked bottle. Cannon hawked phlegm onto the floor.

'Beer?'

The barkeep shook his head. 'Right out, friend. I'm waitin' on a shipment now. Got real good whiskey, though. Made it myself an' the first one's on the house.'

Azul shrugged and picked up the glass. There was a dark tidemark around the inner rim. The whiskey went down hot and fierce: he could feel it burning all the way to his belly, where it seemed to expand and fill his insides with fire. Cannon swallowed his and began to cough noisily. The barkeep tossed his down and watched anxiously.

'Well, gents? What you think?'

'Christ!' Cannon's face was flushed and he was fighting to get his breath. 'What the hell you put in this?'

The barkeep started to list the ingredients, but Cannon waved him to silence, motioning for him to pour a fresh round.

After he had swallowed again he asked, 'You got a bath?'

'Sure.' The man nodded enthusiastically. 'Genuine bath-house out back. Built it myself. Got a place to sleep, too. Sheets ain't been used in a month.'

The bath-house was a lean-to with a sloping roof and sacks hung from a rope across the front. The floor was hard-packed dirt with a metal pump set off to one side. The tub was a huge, ornate affair that the barkeep proudly announced had been brought in at considerable expense from Ogden. There was a spider's web strung dusty from the unconnected spigots and a mess of dead insects around the drain hole. The sleeping quarters consisted of a low-roofed cabin built onto the main body of the saloon. Like the bath-house, the floor was packed dirt, with wooden bunks down both walls and dirty sheets on the beds.

'You build this, too?' Azul asked.

The barkeep nodded. 'Best you'll find in a week's ride.'

'How far's the nearest town?' Azul questioned.

The barkeep grinned and said, 'A week's ride.'

They drank more of the colourless whiskey while the water heated. Then they scrubbed down with gritty soap and doused under the cold water of the pump. When they returned inside the saloon there were five men drinking with the owner. They greeted the two travellers with incurious stares and mumbled welcomes. It was though they had gotten used to living in the middle of nowhere for so long the outside world held no further interest. Cannon ordered food, which was served by a flat-faced Indian woman of unguessable age, her homely face made ugly by two knifecuts that had severed her nostrils. Her breath came in a shrill whistling sound.

'What the hell happened to her face?' Cannon asked.

'Ran away from her husband,' said the barkeep. 'She's a Ute. They cut her to punish her. Real good in bed, though. An' cheap.'

Cannon shook his head and glanced at Azul. 'You want her?'

'No,' answered the halfbreed. 'I want to clap, I'll use my hands.'

The barkeep shrugged like a man long accustomed to refusal.

'Where you headed?' he asked. It was the first sign of interest anyone had shown.

'Place called Clinton,' said Cannon. 'Up near a canyon called Silver Wreath.'

'Ute country.' The barkeep poured them coffee. 'You best watch for a wild injun they call Captain Sam. He raises hell when he's in the mind.'

'How far?' Azul asked.

'A week,' said the man. 'It's that town I was tellin' you about.'

He wandered away to pour drinks and study the cards in the hands of the men clustered around an upturned barrel. The Ute woman took their plates away, favouring

Azul with what might have been intended as a come-hither glance. The halfbreed ignored her and she muttered in guttural English, 'Goddam Apaches. Think they're better than anyone else.' Cannon began to laugh.

They finished the bottle of home-brew and went out to the sleeping cabin. Cannon stretched gratefully on one of the bunks, pleased to be sleeping in a bed. Azul looked at the sheets and felt the straw-filled palliasse beneath: he opted for the floor.

The next day they started out on the final leg of their long journey. A breeze was blowing down from the north, taking the edge off the heat, and that – allied with the proximity of his goal – seemed to revitalise Cannon. The fatigue he had shown back in the Apache country fell away from him. He rode straighter in the saddle and when they halted nights there was less evidence of weariness in his movements. He talked more, telling the halfbreed about his career as a hired gun, even about his dead wife. The only thing he failed to mention was his health. Whether from choice, or simply because he had forgotten the gloomy warnings of the San Antonio doctor, Azul could not tell; nor did he question the old man on the subject. Some things were best left unsaid.

And as the gunfighter's mood brightened, so Azul's grew more sombre.

There was no reason for it, nothing he could clearly define, but the closer they drew to Clinton the more he felt an air of brooding menace. He said nothing to Cannon, not wanting to depress the old man. Not having any reason to disclose a presentiment he could not even explain to himself, he chose to keep it to himself.

He recalled a thing old Sees-Both-Ways, the Chiricahua shaman had once told him. It had been during one of those rambling lessons the old man gave the youths of Azul's *rancheria*, not seeming to have any specific point, but winding gradually to a conclusion that remained with the young halfbreed, buried in his mind until such time as it became relevant.

'There are three kinds of man,' Sees-Both-Ways had said. *'One looks always to the sun. He sees only brightness; hears only the songbirds. He is surprised if the brightness fades. If the sun is hidden behind storm clouds. And then his heart is dark with grief. One sees only the night, lit pale by the moon. He sees the owl – the messenger of death – and he hears only the whisper of the night wind over the grass. Like the voices of the dead not yet gone to the Shadow World. And should the sun strike his face, he is surprised; he does not know what this light is.*

'The third kind is the man who knows there is both sun and moon. Both day and night. That for each owl there is an eagle; that the night wind cools the grass that it may grow richer under the sun. Where the others are like knives with only one cutting edge, this man is a knife with two sides.

'But even he may come to grief. All men seek something. A pony or a woman. A place to live. A child. And when a man wants something hard enough he can forget the whisper in the night. Forget that his knife cuts two ways. He may turn his face to the sun, forgetting that night follows day. And if he does not gain this thing he seeks, then he is like a man who has sought to climb a rocky hill only to find his way barred by stone that he seeks to tear down. And in doing that, he tears the stone down upon himself and is destroyed. The stone is there: the man must go around it to find the sunlight again.'

Azul lay on his blanket watching the clouds scud across the face of the moon. An owl hooted twice, then a third time. A nightjar shrieked its raucous cry. He hoped Abe Cannon would not find a wall of stone barring his way.

Clinton was located at the centre of a broad valley. North and south, timbered hills bulked from an expanse of lush grass, closing in to the east and west so that the town was sheltered from the cold winds that in winter would blow down from the Rockies. Even now, in summer, the farther peaks shone white with snow under the clear blue brilliance of the sky. But the town sat snug, cradled by the hills like a baby surrounded by piled furs against the chilly winds of winter. The buildings ran up against the shores of a lake that reflected back the blueness of the sky so that the surface was a pure azure, clear and smooth as the polished stones Apache women wore as ornaments.

A wide street ran down the middle of the town, flanked by buildings reaching two and three storeys. Most were constructed of timber, wagon trails leading down from the hills where patches of cleared ground showed the source of the building materials; a few were built of stone. At right angles to mainstreet side alleys ran out away from the water, lined with neat-looking houses that sported little gardens and vegetable patches. There was a small church, painted white, with a black tiled roof and a stubby belfry containing a gleaming brass bell. A clapboard livery with a corral out back stood at the western end of mainstreet, beside it a stage depot. There was a general store, a hardware store, a dry goods store and a blacksmith's, the latter giving off a thin column of dark smoke that drifted on the breeze. A millinery occupied a corner position opposite a marshal's office and jailhouse. There was a saloon with a balcony at the front; an eating house; a two-storey hotel; and a whorehouse larger than most of the surrounding structures. The bank was built of stone, with metal bars covering the windows set either side of an imposing wooden door. It was set apart from the buildings either side by alleys running down to the lake.

Clinton looked sleepily prosperous. Like a rich man basking in the sun. There was a rowboat out on the lake, two men dangling poles into the water as they passed a jug between them. Children watched them from the shoreline, racing away as the thunder of hooves and the yelling of the driver announced the arrival of a stage.

'That's it.' Cannon reined in. 'Ain't that just about the sweetest town you ever see?'

'Looks rich,' murmured Azul.

'Yeah.' Cannon wiped dust from his moustache. 'There's a lotta money down there. Good horse country out in the canyons. Good timber in the hills. Warm in winter an' cool in summer. Fishin' if that takes yore fancy. It's a real nice place. Good place for a man to settle down.'

'Silver Wreath,' Azul asked, 'where's that?'

Cannon pointed to where the flanks of the valley curved in over to the east.

'You ride a day beyond the pass, then turn north. You can reach it by noon.'

He leant across in his saddle to slap the halfbreed on the shoulder.

'We'll go in an' get cleaned up. Then we'll take a few drinks an' I'll buy you the best dinner you tasted in weeks. Buy you a girl after, if you want. Hell! I owe you enough.'

'You don't owe me anything,' Azul said.

'Friend,' Cannon grinned, 'way I see it, I owe you my life. Weren't for you, I could be pushing up cactus roses back in Valverde. Or chewin' on my own balls with them Chiricahua brothers of yours. Or I could be coolin' my heels in the Fort Thomas stockade. Christ! Azul, I owe you a lot.'

The halfbreed shrugged. 'I'll settle for the meal and the whiskey. After that, let's see.'

'They're clean.' Cannon winked obscenely. 'The marshal down there's a feller called Heck Thomsett. He runs a tight town. Checks every girl hisself, an' last I saw him he was real healthy.'

'What about Silver Wreath?' asked Azul.

'It ain't goin' away.' Cannon went on smiling. Like a man coming home and taking his time thinking about his welcome; warming himself on the thought. 'Come morning we'll go see Holly in the bank. Get the papers signed. Then we'll ride out there. Tell you something – that stallion o' yours would make fine breeding stock if you want to stick around a spell.'

Azul nodded. 'Sure. He's brought me a long way: he could use pleasuring, too.'

Cannon laughed and dug his heels against the ribs of the bay gelding. Sensing its rider's mood, the big horse took off at a gallop as Cannon threw back his head and let go a high, exuberant yell. Azul gave the grey his head and followed down the slope after the gunfighter.

'That was good.'

Cannon wiped cream from his moustache and picked up his coffee cup. It was a delicate china thing, with a pattern painted on the sides to match the chintzy curtains decorating the windows of the eating house. Azul nodded and pushed his own plate away. He felt vaguely uncomfortable in the surroundings, not used to the accoutrements of luxury the place boasted. The chairs were a little too soft and the atmosphere a little too warm. It was a long time since he'd seen a table covered with a cloth, and back in New Mexico men would have killed for the amount of silver plating the knives and forks and spoons.

'All right,' Cannon said, 'let's go get that drink.'

Azul nodded and climbed to his feet, ignoring the curious stares of the other diners as he settled the Sonoran stetson on his mane of sun-bleached hair. As he went out the waitress who had served them smiled at him. This time he smiled back: she was a good-looking woman.

The saloon was called The Traveller's Rest. It was big and bright and noisy. A brass foot rail ran the length of a long mahogany bar, flanked at intervals by polished brass spittoons. A gigantic mirror hung on one wall, reflecting the painting of a massively-breasted woman with flaming red hair and a twist of white material between her thighs that hung above the bar. The air was aromatic with cigar smoke and loud with the chinking of glasses. A piano and banjo were drumming out a tune at the far end of the room; a line of six girls in bright red costumes cut low at the front and flounced in back was fighting to keep time with the music.

Cannon shouted for whiskey and two glasses. As the barkeep poured he asked, 'Ain't Heck Thomsett around?'

The barkeep was half Cannon's age. A smooth-faced young man with elastic suspenders holding the sleeves of his striped shirt off his wrists. He looked at Cannon with a curious frown.

'You ain't heard?'

'I guess not.' The grey-haired man tossed down his drink. Poured himself another. 'Why don't you tell me?'

'He got shot.' The barkeep drew a mug of beer. Swallowed. 'Couple o' kids tried to pull a job on Holly's bank. Heck went up against them. They all lost. Heck was getting old, I guess.'

'Yeah.' Cannon's exuberance left him suddenly. 'Ain't we all? Pore old Heck. He had guts.'

'Yeah, he did.' The barkeep emptied his mug. 'I saw them. One o' the kids was carryin' a scattergun.'

Cannon's face went pale under the tan. For a moment he looked his full age. Like a man who feels the first stone come loose in his hand.

CHAPTER ELEVEN

Ben Holly was a short, fat man with the kind of face that looked a stranger to the sun. He was very pink, a wispy circle of pale yellow hair surrounding the shiny dome of his skull. His features were small, the eyes and nose and mouth not large enough to balance the surrounding flesh. His hands were tiny, delicate; with small, thin fingers that ended in neatly-manicured, very white nails. The hardest thing about him was his stare: his eyes were black, lustrous as a beetle's carapace, and very alert.

As Cannon and Azul entered his office he removed a pair of gold half-frame spectacles from the bridge of his foreshortened nose and set them neatly on the massive desk. He was wearing a pale grey suit, a white shirt that looked too tight around his fleshy neck, and a pale grey necktie with a silver pattern. He had kept them waiting outside the better part of an hour, and when he rang the little silver bell on his desk to bid them enter, the guard who stood by his door came in with them.

'Nothing personal.' His voice was like his face: soft and smooth. 'But since the robbery.' He corrected himself with a nervous laugh. 'Since the *attempted* robbery . . . Well, I have to be careful. You understand?'

Cannon nodded, taking the small, limp hand the banker extended. As Holly leant across the desk to shake, his belly sagged over the edge. He nodded, wiping his hands together, and motioned for them to sit down. The guard stayed by the door, his face blank, the Winchester carbine he carried cradled in his arms.

'Mister . . .?' Holly peered at the gunfighter.

'Cannon. Abe Cannon.'

'Ah, yes.' Holly opened a drawer in his desk to fetch a file out. 'And Mister . . .?'

'Gunn,' supplied Azul. 'Matthew Gunn.'

'You're partners?' Holly asked, glancing from one man to the other.

'Yeah,' said Cannon. 'Something like that.'

Holly opened the file, settling the spectacles back on his nose. His lips moved slightly as he read. They looked like two worms copulating.

'Yes.' He left the file open in front of him. 'Silver Wreath canyon. A deposit of two hundred and fifty dollars. With interest that makes three hundred and seventy five. A respectable sum.'

Cannon dropped a leather satchel on the desk.

'There's nine hundred in there. That an' what I already paid you makes –.' He paused, frowning as he began to calculate.

'One thousand, two hundred and seventy five,' Holly said. 'A substantial amount.'

'Enough to buy me Silver Wreath an' leave some over to get started,' said Cannon.

'Yes.' Holly removed the spectacles and dabbed at his mouth with a silk kerchief. It was the same colour as his suit. 'Have you thought of investing it? I can guarantee you a handsome return. Easily enough to live on.'

Cannon frowned. 'I already invested it. In Silver Wreath. I'm gonna raise horses.'

'Excellent horse country.' Holly nodded. 'Excellent. If it weren't for the Indians . . .'

'We can handle them,' said Cannon. 'I got no quarrel with them.'

'Captain Sam.' Holly glanced at the guard. 'He's been giving trouble lately.'

'Look.' Cannon sounded impatient now. 'I don't know nothing about this Captain Sam, but I just come through Apache country to settle down here. I ain't about to change my mind on account o' no Ute.'

'Yes. I see.' Holly looked down at the file. Then at Cannon. Then at the guard. 'But still . . .'

'But nothing!' Cannon cut across the banker. 'I put down a deposit an' I got yore paper. The land deed. You give me yore word to hold Silver Wreath for me. Now I come to collect. Full title to the canyon.'

Holly mopped his mouth again. The sun coming in through the window behind him reflected off his spectacles. Glinting like Azul's mirror signals.

'There's the problem, Mister Cannon. The *full* title. You don't have the *full* title.'

'I got yore word on it.' Cannon reached inside his black coat. 'Here.'

Holly took the paper. He said, 'Yes. My receipt for your deposit. I undertook to hold your money against possession of Silver Wreath canyon. Subject to . . .'

'Subject to my givin' you the rest,' interrupted Cannon. 'Like we agreed.'

Holly turned the paper round so that the words faced the gunfighter. A pink nail tapped a section of small print at the bottom.

'Subject to current land prices and the continuing availability of the section in question,' he said formally. 'That's the problem.'

'There ain't no problem,' Cannon snapped. 'We agreed it. You give me yore word.'

'To hold the canyon for you if I *could*,' said Holly. 'That was some years ago, Mister Cannon.'

'Man's word is his word,' said the gunfighter. 'You telling me I don't own the canyon?'

Holly smiled nervously. He touched the knot of his tie.

'In a nutshell, Mister Cannon: yes. Clinton has grown since you were last here. There've been settlers coming in from the East. Land prices have rocketed.'

The creases in Cannon's face got deeper as his jaw tightened. His eyes got cold. Azul saw the stones shift, coming loose. Cannon stared at the banker.

'You bastard! You sold it.'

Holly shrugged. 'I'm a businessman, Mister Cannon. My business is making money.'

'Who's got it?' The gunfighter's voice was a mixture of rage and worry. There was fear in it: the fear of a man who sees the rock barrier shift to block out the sun. 'Who you sell it to?'

'Actually.' Holly's eyes shifted from Cannon to Azul to the guard. 'I own it.'

'Jesus!' The fury was open now in Cannon's voice. 'You tellin' me you took my money an' then bought Silver Wreath yoreself?'

Holly nodded. 'Yes, Mister Cannon. It was too good a deal to overlook.'

The tendons in the gunfighter's neck stood out corded against the skin. His right elbow moved to shove back the hem of his coat, clearing his holster. His hand closed on the butt of the Peacemaker. Behind him the guard's Winchester clicked as the hammer went back.

'Abe!' Azul cautioned.

Cannon's hand came slowly clear of the gun. His face was pale.

'You can't do that,' he said gruffly. 'It ain't right.'

Holly shrugged again. 'Right, Mister Cannon?' His voice was unctuous. 'This is business.'

'I'll kill you.' Now Cannon's voice was flat; cold and hard. 'Silver Wreath is mine.'

'I don't carry a gun.' As Holly said it, the guard moved away from the door, the carbine swinging to cover Cannon. 'But Springsteen does.'

Cannon stood up. He lifted the leather satchel from the desk with his left hand. Picked up the paper.

'I'm gonna leave these with the marshal, Holly. Then I'm goin' out to Silver Wreath an' start buildin' my spread. That canyon's mine. We made a deal an' by God! you're gonna stick to it. You best change them papers of yours. The money'll be waitin' for you.'

'You don't understand,' said Holly. A faint sheen of perspiration covered his face. He looked like an ageing baby, fresh from a bath. 'Business isn't like that.'

'Fuck business!' Cannon swung round. The guard stepped back, the Winchester pointed at the old man's belly. Cannon glared at him. 'Springsteen? Next time you point a gun at me, you best use it. Else I'll kill you.'

Springsteen's face didn't alter. Under a mop of tangled dark hair it just looked contemptuous.

'You want I should gun him, Mister Holly?'

Azul moved then. He was already on his feet, but now he took a step forwards. The movement caught Springsteen's attention and he turned slightly, the muzzle of the carbine shifting to point at the halfbreed.

Azul closed the distance between them before the Winchester was lined. His right hand took the barrel, pushing it down as his left swung round, the palm landing open on the guard's cheek. The Winchester blasted a slug into the front of Holly's desk. Azul's knee came up, driving hard into Springsteen's groin. The sallow face sucked in, turning pale as the man groaned and doubled over. Azul tore the carbine from his hands. Began to work the lever, sending shells in a golden shower over the curled-up body as the door opened and a second guard pulled up short on the muzzle of Cannon's pistol.

Holly said, 'It's all right, Caleb. Just a disagreement. Business.'

Azul dropped the Winchester. 'Let's go, Abe.'

'Yeah.' Cannon holstered the Colt. 'This place stinks.'

'I'll hold it for you, but I don't know you got any right to the canyon.'

The marshal was younger than Cannon, older than Azul. His hair was black, slicked over in a tidy parting held in place with a pomade that gave off a faint, sweetish odour. His lips were thin and straight beneath a hawkish nose, his eyes somewhere between green and grey. He wore a Merwin & Hulbert Pocket Army revolver in a shoulder rig.

'You seen the paper,' said Cannon. 'You seen my money.'

The peace officer shrugged. His name was Winston Murdoch and he knew Ben Holly was a whole lot bigger around Clinton than Abe Cannon.

'Ain't my line of business. Thing like this, you need a court to decide.'

'You got a court?' Cannon asked.

Murdoch shook his head. 'Not in Clinton. Got a Citizens Committee. Ben Holly's the chairman. Big things, they get settled by the Territorial Judge. He'll be comin' by in a few months.'

'I ain't waitin' a few months,' grunted Cannon. 'I'm goin' out to Silver Wreath now. Holly knows the money's here, he wants to pick it up.'

Murdoch shrugged again. 'I got no jurisdiction outside the town limits, Cannon. You want to ride out to Silver Wreath, that's yore business. I can't stop you. You start anything in Clinton, though, that's somethin' else.'

'I ain't startin' anything,' said Cannon. 'I'm finishin' something.'

Murdoch raised his eyebrows. 'You got my receipt. I'll hold yore money until it's settled.'

He watched as they went out the door. Then he stood up and stepped onto the sidewalk, waiting until he saw them ride down the street, heading eastwards in the direction of the canyon. When they were out of sight he settled a black, straight-brim stetson on his head and hurried over to the bank.

'Well,' Cannon spread his arms as though seeking to embrace the canyon. 'What you think?'

Azul stared round. Silver Wreath was an almost perfect circle, banded by a ring of wooded hills that lifted in gentle folds to the steeper ground beyond. Off in the distance a waterfall splashed down a face of sheer rock, pooling at the bottom and then running out into a wide, shallow stream that was flanked by willows. The grass was thick and lush, very green in the afternoon sun. Mustangs grazed around the pool, the stallion watching guardedly over his brood mares.

'It's a good place,' said the halfbreed. 'Like you said.'

'Ain't it just?' grinned Cannon. 'An' I got it all figgered out.'

He began to point, showing where he planned to build his cabin; where he would erect a corral. Azul listened with the sense of foreboding growing stronger: the stones were very loose now.

'We'll buy some mules.' Cannon was enthusiastic, seeing only the sun shining on the good grass, on the good earth. Not seeing the shadow. 'To haul timber. Need axes, too. Saws. I got it all worked out.'

'And Holly?' asked the halfbreed. 'He could start trouble.'

'Holly?' Cannon spat on the grass. 'That'll be the day.'

CHAPTER TWELVE

Azul wiped sweat from his face and tied the bandanna back around his mane of pale hair. He lifted the axe and began to swing the heavy blade against the tree. Chips flew as the cut grew deeper and soon the trunk began to bend over, a groaning sound creaking from the timber. He stepped clear, watching as the pine toppled, crashing onto the grass. Deftly, he set to trimming off the branches, setting aside those large enough to be useful and piling the kindling to one side for a later gathering.

His torso gleamed in the sunlight, the oath scars that latticed his left arm pale on the deep tan of his naked skin. He fastened a rope around the trunk and picked up the reins of the mule team, whooping the long-eared animals into pace as they hauled the log down the slope to Silver Wreath. A track was already gouged out, leading down and across the grass to where the beginnings of a cabin were outlined, close to the waterfall. The floor was down and the walls were now jutting a good three feet above the ground. A big black stove stood at one corner, its tall metal chimney supported by poles, and under a tarpaulin the outlines of chairs and a table and a bed were visible. Across the pool formed by the outspill of the falls there was a corral, inside which the grey stallion and Cannon's bay grazed contentedly. Cannon looked up as the halfbreed approached, setting down the saw he was using to come up and help with the log.

They had been in the canyon almost a month, living out of a lean-to as they worked on the corral and the feeder shute and the cabin. There had been no further word from Holly, nor any sign that he intended to give them trouble. They had gone into Clinton several times, purchasing the mules and the tools and supplies, and beyond a surly look from Springsteen there had been no evidence that the banker intended to do more than sit back and leave them to work. He had not collected the money from Murdoch and Cannon had decided he was waiting for the Territorial Judge to arrive. The gunfighter was confident that any court would find in his favour: after all, he had Holly's paper and possession was nine tenths of the law.

Azul was less confident. The feeling of foreboding remained with him, combined with puzzlement at his own motives. Imbued as he was with the free spirit of the Chiricahua, he saw no point to building anything so permanent as the cabin. The canyon was everything Cannon had said: fodder-rich and well-watered, sheltered by the surrounding hills where game was to be had for the asking. A man could easily live there throughout the hot months of summer without need of more shelter than the trees, chasing in and breaking the wild mustangs. They could be sold off for whatever supplies a man would need, and when the cold weather came he could move south, following the sun until it came time to return again. But the white side of his nature told him that such a nomadic existence was not enough for Cannon. The old man wanted to put roots down before he died; wanted a place he could call his own. Wanted somewhere to die. And so Azul stayed, ignoring that part of his nature that told him it was not needful to claim the land, working alongside Cannon to give the gunfighter his dream.

For no reason he could define he felt he owed Cannon that much.

'We're pretty low on salt an' flour,' Cannon remarked when they had the log set for trimming. 'Think I'll ride in to Clinton come morning.'

Azul nodded. 'Want me along?'

'As you like.' Cannon splashed water in his face. 'Don't reckon I'll run into nothing I can't handle.'

'I'll hunt.' Azul felt no particular desire to visit the

town, and there were deer in the hills. 'Get us some meat.'

'Right.' Cannon grinned, massaging the small of his back. 'I'll fetch some whiskey. We can have an early house warming.'

It was late afternoon when Abe Cannon rode into Clinton. The sun was shining on his face and he was looking forward to spending time in the saloon and maybe later paying a visit to the whorehouse. It had been a long time.

He checked the gelding into the livery and paced down the street to The Traveller's Rest. He was coming up to the batwings when they swung outwards as Springsteen and the guard called Caleb came through. Both men had been drinking. Cannon could smell it on their breath and see it in their eyes. He stepped back, instinct dropping his right hand close to the butt of the Peacemaker.

Springsteen looked at him and sneered.

'Well, look what we got here.' His voice was nasal; whiney. 'That famous old gunfighter. *Mister* Abe Cannon.'

Beside him, Caleb sniggered.

Cannon paused. Both men were wearing sidearms. Springsteen had a Colt's Peacemaker on his right hip, Caleb was wearing twinned Remingtons cross-hung around his thick waist. They halted facing him, lips curled.

'He don't look much of a gunfighter to me,' said Caleb. 'Looks kinda like some old man don't have the sense to know when he's licked.'

'Careful,' warned Springsteen, joking. 'I hear he was real bigtime. Once.'

'Musta been a long time ago,' sniggered Caleb. 'Before his brain got addled.'

Cannon moved to the batwings, not wanting trouble. Not with his dream at stake. Springsteen's hand came out, blocking his way.

'How's that cabin comin' on?' he asked. 'You an' the halfbreed got it finished yet?'

'Real nice of him to build Mister Holly a cabin,' said Caleb. 'Get everything fixed up ready for us.'

'Get outta my way.' Cannon's voice was hard now: stripping off the years.

Springsteen moved to block the gates. 'Make me.'

'I give you one warning,' said Cannon. 'You don't get a second.'

Springsteen stared at him for what seemed like a long time. Then, 'You gonna make me, old man? You ain't the 'breed to do yore fightin' now.'

Cannon had seen that look too many times before. Heard that tone too many times. Now there was no backing off. No way out or around. Just the one way: forwards. There was no choice now.

He sighed. 'You want to try it on yore own, boy? Or you need yore friend to side you?'

'Hell!' Springsteen chuckled. 'I don't need no help to take an old has-been like you.'

Cannon stepped off the sidewalk without taking his eyes from Springsteen's angular face. His elbow hiked back the tail of his coat as he positioned himself so that the sun was on his back. It was warm. He hoped it was the heat that was making him sweat: he wished he could take just one drink. Then Springsteen stepped down onto the street and he pushed everything from his mind, the way he had so many times before, concentrating on the one thing that was going to happen now. Here. No more talking. No more prodding. Just him and a man young enough to be his son. If he'd ever had a son.

'Call it,' said Springsteen.

And drew.

He was fast. A natural. Nearly as good as Cannon had been at his age. He fisted the Colt from the holster with his thumb taking the hammer back, getting his forefinger down on the trigger as he cleared leather.

Cannon saw the pistol coming up as though in slow motion. It had always been like that for him: as if time slowed and he had all the time in the world to draw his own gun. When he was young. Before age and whatever that funny-sounding illness the San Antonio doctor had told him he had slowed him down. For an instant that lasted an eternity it was like the old days. He was young again and the weight of the Peacemaker was familiar in his hand, the butt roughened just enough it wouldn't slide on a sweat-slickened palm. The trigger smooth. The cross-hatching of the hammer rough under the callous of his thumb. He heard the familiar triple *click!* as the hammer came back. Felt the faint connection of pins, the pressure of the spring. Smelled the old, friendly reek of the black powder smoke. Felt the Colt buck in his hand.

And knew he wasn't young any more.

Knew he wasn't the best any more.

He felt something pluck at his left side. Felt his legs go out from under him.

Oh, Jesus! he thought. Not knowing if he was praying or blaspheming. I'm hit. The little bastard's shot me.

There was a film of light over his eyes. It was bright and he wasn't sure whether it was the sun or muzzle flash or tears. Then he smiled, because Springsteen was down on his back, his shoulders resting against the sidewalk. His dark eyes were wide and staring, his mouth hanging open. There was a big red patch spreading over his shirt, just above the belt. At its centre there was a neat, round hole that oozed a steady pulsing of bright crimson. His hand was empty now, the Colt down in the dust too far away for his scrabbling fingers to reach it. He pushed forwards, stretching out his arm. He was weeping and shaking his head. Then, with that abruptness that comes as death closes the final shutter on a man's life, Springsteen jerked rigid. His fingers almost touched the gun before his body shuddered and a choking, wracking gargle erupted from his slack mouth. He fell back, eyes staring up at a sky he could no longer see.

Shit! Cannon thought. I ain't so slow after all. I didn't do so bad. Not for an old man.

He pushed up on his hands and knees, suddenly aware that a fire was burning in his left side. He shook his head, watching Caleb. The other man was staring at him with his mouth hanging open and fear in his eyes. Cannon became aware he was pointing the Colt, the hammer primed for a second shot. Then he realised something hot and salty was filling his throat. It seemed to come up from inside him, from where the fire was burning. It choked him and he began to cough, seeing the bright red spots of blood splatter onto the dust. Splatter over his shirt. He stood up. Slowly. Painfully. Not sure if he was lung-shot, or if something had just burst inside him.

He saw Ben Holly come out of the saloon. Saw the banker's mouth form words he couldn't hear. Saw Winston Murdoch come running along the street.

Saw Caleb nod in answer to whatever it was the banker was saying.

And knew he had been set up.

He triggered the Peacemaker as Caleb drew the matched Remingtons. The guard was hurled back by the force of the slug that hit his chest and Cannon realised his hand was shaking because the bullet had been aimed at Caleb's belly. He always aimed for the belly: that way a man was hurt too bad to fight even if the shot missed the vital organs.

Caleb slammed back against the frontage of The Traveller's Rest with his eyes closed and his hands thrust out in front. He was wearing a black vest, so it was hard to see the blood bursting from his ruptured heart. It was clearer on his face: pain had robbed that of colour and the crimson gouting from his mouth shone bright in the sun, against the sudden pallor. He struck the woodwork and slid down onto the sidewalk. He left a long smear. Like an exclamation mark.

Holly was bending down now, trying to prise the Remington from Caleb's left hand. Cannon thumbed the Colt's hammer back. It seemed to take a long time.

Murdoch shouted, 'Ben! Don't!' He had the Merwin & Hulbert out from the shoulder rig. It was pointing at Cannon.

He said, 'He's dying. Jesus Christ! Ben, he's already dead.'

Holly let go the Remington. He had broken Caleb's trigger finger trying to grab it. He looked at Cannon. Nodded. Then he disappeared inside the saloon like a frightened jackrabbit bolting into its hole.

Cannon coughed some more. Spat blood that puddled in the dust. It looked very bright.

Murdoch said, 'Put the gun away, Cannon.'

The old man shook his head. It was curiously hard to form words through the thickness in his mouth.

'It's over.' Murdoch pointed at Caleb. At Springsteen.

'The price you pay.' Cannon looked at the bodies. 'They weren't fast enough.'

'Enough,' Murdoch grunted. 'It's over.'

Cannon nodded. The fire was worse now. It was hard to breathe. He took a step backwards, still holding the Peacemaker on Murdoch. Then his feet seemed to tangle and he toppled over. The Colt flew from his hand, the hammer tripping so that a slug blasted splinters from the sidewalk.

Murdoch said, 'Christ!' and holstered the bulldog pistol. He looked at Cannon stretched on the street, wondering how the old man was still moving with that amount of blood spilling out of his mouth and side. He said, 'Somebody go fetch his horse.'

They brought the bay gelding from the livery and lifted Abe Cannon into the saddle. Murdoch emptied the Peacemaker and pushed it down into the holster. Ben Holly came back out of the saloon and watched as they tied Cannon's ankles to the stirrups, his wrists to the saddlehorn. Murdoch led the horse down mainstreet and pointed its head in the direction of Silver Wreath. Then he slapped his hat hard over the bay's flanks and watched the big horse run.

Back in The Traveller's Rest Ben Holly bought the marshal a drink.

'I imagine that settles it,' he murmured. 'A dead man can't claim land.'

'No.' Murdoch put his glass down untouched : suddenly he had no taste for Holly's whiskey. 'You set this up, Ben?'

Holly just smiled. An innocent, baby-faced smile. All creased pink flesh and neat, white teeth.

Azul saw the bay coming as he butchered the deer. He wiped the Bowie knife on the grass and sank his bloody arms into the stream. Then he frowned and began to lope forwards to meet the horse.

His face set into harsh lines when he saw Cannon's body. The front of the old man's shirt was dark with drying blood. It was crusted over his jaw, the fresher streaming from his mouth leaving thin lines of scarlet that contrasted with the older, darker crimson. Flies buzzed in the still air as the halfbreed cut the ropes holding Cannon in place and lifted him gently down. His eyes were open, staring unseeing at Azul's face.

'Tell me how,' Azul murmured. 'How'd it happen?'

Cannon made a noise deep in his throat.

'Abe!' Azul cradled the dying man's head. 'Listen to me. Take your time, but tell me who did it.'

The rattling noise became a name, 'Springsteen.'

Cannon smiled, cracking encrusted blood. 'I got him. Him an' Caleb.'

Azul brushed a fly from Cannon's mouth, 'I'll fetch you a drink.'

'It's too late.' Cannon touched Azul's hand. 'I'm finished. Holly set it up. Right down the line. I guess I don't get to raise horses after all.'

Moisture oozed from the corners of his eyes.

'Bury me here. Please. I come here to die.'

'Sure.' Azul nodded, not certain Cannon could hear him any longer: the stones were tumbled now, fallen down and piling over the body, cutting off the sun forever. 'Then I'll settle the debts.'

A long, harsh breath whistled from Cannon's mouth. It smelled of something rotten. His shoulders slumped and Azul felt the life go out of him. He let the head down carefully onto the grass and climbed to his feet. The bay gelding watched him nervously as he looked around Silver

Wreath canyon. It was just a place now. Nowhere special, just one more canyon in Utah where an old man had wanted to breed horses. Maybe someone else would, someday. But not Ben Holly. No: not Ben Holly.

Azul fetched a shovel and dug a grave close to the waterfall. He cleaned Cannon's body and lowered it into the hole. There was no marker: just a mound of turned soil. He took the saddle off the bay and turned it loose. Then he opened the corral so the mules could wander free. After that he gathered what few things he needed and climbed up on the grey stallion, turning the pony's head towards the entrance, riding in the direction of Clinton.

There was one last promise he needed to fulfil.

A final debt to settle. The Apache way.

Murdoch looked up as the halfbreed came into the office. He pushed back his chair, folding his arms across his chest to get his right hand near the Merwin & Hulbert.

'Cannon's dead,' said Azul.

'I figgered,' said Murdoch. 'He was dyin' when I sent him out.'

'His money?' Azul asked. 'You still got that?'

The marshal nodded. 'You was his partner. I guess it goes to you now.'

'No.' Azul shook his head. 'I told him I didn't want money. That's not important. Just see the judge decides where it goes.'

Murdoch nodded again. 'You? I don't want no trouble.'

'No trouble,' murmured Azul. 'I'm going back south.'

He turned and went out of the office. Behind him, Murdoch sighed: he was glad the 'breed hadn't started something. He wasn't sure he could handle it.

Azul walked his horse slowly down mainstreet. It was close to evening and the stores were closing down. Children were running home to dinner and the town was emptying out. It still looked rich. Placid as the waters of the lake that now glittered blood red in the setting sun.

The stone frontage of the bank was a ruddy hue, the barred windows shuttered against the encroaching night. He turned into one of the alleys flanking the building and rode down to the water's edge. Willows banded the shore here and he dismounted, tethering the grey in the shadows amongst the trees. He left the Sonoran stetson hung on the saddle and fastened the leather band the Chiricahua warriors wore in battle around his hair. Then he walked back towards mainstreet.

Lights were going on, but the alley was dark; deserted save for a red and white dog that growled softly as he went by. He flattened against the wall, hidden in shadow as he listened for the sound of the big door closing.

There was the thud of wood on metal. The scrape of a key.

Ben Holly's voice said, 'Good night,' and footsteps echoed on the sidewalk. Azul watched him go by : a short, plump figure, the frizz of golden hair hidden under a grey derby.

And he said softly, 'Holly.'

The banker paused. 'Who's that?'

Azul came out of the shadows. Holly started back, but the halfbreed's hand reached out to grab the folds of the banker's coat and haul him into the alley. His left hand clamped hard over the smooth, pink cheeks, the fingers digging viciously into the soft flesh. Holly whimpered, his beetle-black eyes getting huge. Fear spread a stain of urine across the front of his pants.

'You killed Abe Cannon.' Azul's voice was harsh, the accents of his Chiricahua blood foremost now. 'You set it up.'

He took his hand from the banker's mouth.

Holly said, 'Springsteen did it,' in a thin, shrill voice.

'But you set it up,' Azul rasped. 'Why?'

Holly looked into the pale blue eyes and saw death there. He began to tremble.

'I checked it,' he stuttered, spittle flecking his lips. 'I wondered why they called it Silver Wreath.'

Azul dragged him deeper into the alley. Deeper into the shadows.

'Why did they?' he asked in the same harsh tone.

'The Utes.' The banker was trembling uncontrollably now. 'They found silver there. Behind the waterfall. That's why I wanted it. Why I left it so long – I didn't want a rush.'

'Who else knows?' Azul grated.

'No one.' Holly shook his head. 'Springsteen knew. Now there's only you. We can share it. I'll make you rich.'

'Holly,' snarled Azul, 'it doesn't matter any more.'

The banker opened his mouth to scream as Azul slid the Bowie knife from the sheath, but the halfbreed's left hand came up again to block off his cries. He raised the knife, holding it in front of the man's face. Holly's eyes stared at the polished steel. They were no longer alert. Only terrified; hypnotised. Like the eyes of a rabbit staring at a fox.

Azul brought the blade forwards and across. It slid over the soft flesh of the banker's throat. Cut down and through. The pink flesh parted: twin lips of bright red pouted. Blood flowed, spoiling Holly's shirt. Fouling his necktie. The gristle of the windpipe gleamed briefly grey, then was lost beneath the crimson. Azul cut again and the windpipe severed. He let go of Holly's face and stood back as the fat man fell to his knees. A gurgling, bubbling sound came from the cut. Holly pressed both hands tight against the wound. Blood spurted from between his clutching fingers. The pinkness went out of his face and his eyes bulged as he fought for the breath – the life – that was leaking out through the great slash in his neck. His eyes bulged.

'They called him Honest Abe,' Azul said, 'because he always told a man when he was going to kill him. He made you that promise. I'm keeping it for him.'

He watched as Holly's eyes glazed over, his face impassive. The banker's hands fell away from his neck and a great spurt of crimson jetted out. Holly's mouth stretched wide. The bubbling sound died away to a wheezing and the fat man went down on his hands. Blood gouted over the dust of the alley. Then his arms gave way and he fell onto his face. His body twitched, feet and fingers digging into the ground. Crimson pooled under his face.

Then the wheezing stopped and the body jerked once and was still. Azul turned away, walking down the alley to where the grey horse was tethered. Behind him, the red and white dog came out from under the bank and began to tear at Holly's neck.

Azul got up on the stallion and settled the stetson back over his mane of sun-bleached hair. The dog was snarling now. There was the sticky, soggy sound of rending flesh. Azul rode south.

AUTHOR'S NOTE

Before anyone says, 'He got the Buddy Holly lines from George G. Gilman,' let me confess : yes, I did. But George and I are the best of friends, and I know he won't mind. I hope no one else does. After all, just because George got there first I don't see why he should keep the edge.

All right?

James A. Muir.
1981.

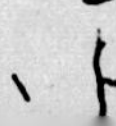